The angry message removed any doubt: Alana knew her life was in danger.

Alana's voice was strident with terror.

"Mark, it's me, Alana!...I'm being harassed, getting crank calls. There've been unpleasant happenings in my life. Bill plans to take me to a safe place. I—we—thought I'd be safe. But...but the man called back, and he's on his way to get me—"

"Calm down, dear," Mark said. "I'll call 9-1-1. You're going to be okay. You have a good security system. Don't unlock for anyone!"

"I won't!" she vowed, even as she heard what sounded like keys being tested in the locks. "Wait—Mark, he's trying keys in my locks!"

"Easy, Lannie. Chances of someone having the right combination for all of your locks are almost nil. Do you have a chain lock on your door?"

"Oh, no! I forgot to hook that!" Alana cried.

She dropped the receiver, ran to the door and at that instant the series of locks lined up, the handle rotated, and the door swung open.... Alana looked up into a sinister face made even more terrifying because it was covered with a woman's black nylon stocking....

"No! Please!" Alana cried as her attacker wrestled with her.

He clamped a foul-smelling cloth across her face. Even as she struggled, she felt her mind being pulled down, down, down into a dark abyss.

BRENDA BANCROFT is a pen name of inspirational romance author Susan Feldhake. At home in central Illinois with her husband, Steven, and four children, she is employed as a writing instructor for a college-accredited correspondence school. In her spare time she likes to hike, listen to country and western music, and fellowship with friends.

Books by Brenda Bancroft

HEARTSONG PRESENTS

HP22—Indy Girl

ROMANCE READER—TWO BOOKS IN ONE (Under the pen name Susan Feldhake)

RR7—For Love Alone & Love's Sweet Promise

A Love
Meant to Be

Brenda Bancroft

Heartsong Presents

ISBN 1-55748-403-1

A LOVE MEANT TO BE

PRINTED IN THE U.S.A.

one

When the telephone on the desk beside her shrilled, Alana Charles was tempted to let the machine take it. She glanced at the clock above the door across the room. It was still early. Nowhere close to business hours. People didn't tend to phone a shop that was not open.

Please don't let it be him, she thought, hoping against hope that it was not the stranger who had taken to calling her at home and even a few times at the boutique when she had been working late into the night.

And then there had been the notes. If they had been sent through the mail, she would probably have turned them over to the window clerks and asked for an appointment with a postal inspector. But they had been shoved under her door.

Was there someone in her apartment complex who wanted her attention? Or might it just be bored teenagers, blissfully unaware that while they laughed, another turned away, brushing tears of fright?

Alana hung in indecision until the fourth ring. Following it, the answering machine automatically picked up.

"The Shoestring Boutique," she answered, grateful that

her voice revealed none of her trepidation.

"Oh, great! I caught you." The reassuring voice of her partner, Carrie McFarlane, eased Alana's tension. "I had a hunch that I would. You're such a workaholic."

"It takes one to know one, my dear," Alana replied, laughing as she leaned back in the plush, swivel chair behind the large desk that almost dwarfed the office area of their shop. The two young women had located their business on a downtown corner of bustling Maple Grove, a bedroom community near St. Louis, Missouri.

Slim, tall, and tanned, Alana sifted her long, baby-fine golden hair through her artfully manicured nails, stifling a yawn as she listened to Carrie explain that her pastor had called about a family moving from the West Coast to the East who'd had trouble on Interstate 70. The family faced travel time lost to breakdowns, and needed temporary shelter and food as their funds were running low and they had three small children to provide for.

"You're sure you don't mind if I'm a little late today, Lana?" Carrie breathlessly inquired.

"It's perfectly all right. A piece of cake. Take your time. Those poor people need you more than I do. Heaven knows you've been there often enough for me in my times of need!"

"You're a dear," Carrie sighed, her tone warm with friendly appreciation. "I'll tell you all about it after I help the pastor make arrangements. We've already got a mechanic willing to work after-hours at his regular wage. We couldn't find anyone else willing to tackle the job on such short notice. Mechanics are like doctors and dentists— they're booked ahead for weeks!"

"You're a true miracle worker, Carrie," Alana teased. "Have you got a couple for me?"

"I wish I did," she bantered back. "Sometimes I think it'd take a pocketful of miracles to make you truly happy."

Alana frowned, her brows furrowing in consternation. She'd always been careful to keep a smile on her face, but evidently her business partner had guessed her deepest, darkest secrets: that she was lonely, and that even though she had so much, she did not know true joy or happiness.

"Sometimes I think it'd take a basketful of miracles to get you a social life again," Carrie went on. "My boyfriend's got any number of acquaintances and colleagues—up-standing business people, well-educated, committed Christians—who'd *love* to go out with you. But all you think about is business, business, *business*!"

"So?" Alana asked, hoping she didn't sound as defensive as she suddenly felt. But the fact that Carrie had included the label "Christian," as if it were a shining attribute, set Alana's teeth on edge.

Not that she had anything against God or religion or church attendance. She didn't. She usually found a pleasant church to attend on Easter and Christmas. But Alana didn't want, or need, spiritual issues to get any more personal than that.

"So what?" Carrie interrupted Alana's musings. "So there's more to life than the bottom line, profit and loss margins, inventorying, and buying trips—"

"No kidding?" Alana said, chuckling. "I didn't know that. Tell me more—but some day when we're not both pressed for time."

"It's a date, pal," Carrie promised, and gave a pseudo-exasperated sigh. "Maybe it's high time that I did just that. There are lots of things as important, and some things way more important, than the business world and balances in various bank accounts, and a new community theater production to perform in every season—"

"Such as?" Alana prompted, even when a sensation at the base of her stomach told her that she shouldn't open the door to Carrie's philosophical ideas.

"Let me see. Faith. Forgiveness. Eternal assurance. True love. Spreading the Good News. Service to others—"

Alana pointedly cleared her throat. "All very interesting, my dear, but a glance at ye olde clock on the wall tells me that I'd better let you go or I'll detain you from serving others, and I'm not sure that they'll forgive me in this lifetime, or the next, if that should happen—"

Alana issued a quick goodbye and hung up the receiver. She looked around the thriving boutique, a specialty store that had done better than their wildest expectations. Alana viewed this fact as something that might slip away as quickly as it had arrived—through a whimsical turn of fate. Carrie, on the other hand, trusted their business would be preserved if the girls both lived their lives and conducted business in a godly, ethical manner, trying to do what the Lord would want in every situation.

Carrie was right about serving others, Alana decided, as she got up from her desk and unlocked the front doors, even though it was a few minutes before nine. If there were shoppers out before the official opening, who was she to deny them a chance to spend their money? The bottom line could always use it!

Carrie was right, too, in that the business was all that Alana had in her life. But if she had too little in her life, Carrie McFarlane seemed to have entirely too much in hers.

Somehow—and Alana wasn't sure how the young woman managed it—Carrie was able to tirelessly serve the needs of others, enjoy a thriving social life, sing in the church choir, serve as secretary for women's circle meetings, date a really neat lawyer, keep in close contact with both her biological family and her church family, and still mother-hen Alana about the supposed lacks that Carrie feared were creating voids in Alana's life.

The girls, in many ways, were as different as day and night, with Carrie as dark-haired as Alana was fair. Carrie was as generous-to-a-fault as Alana was profit-motivated.

Carrie was as committed to everything as Alana was naturally hesitant. But then Carrie hadn't experienced the devastating pain of love as Alana had.

And, while the girls were opposites in many ways, in others they were duplicates—a fact that made it easy for them to get along both as business partners and friends. With what remained of Alana's relatives so far away, both geographically and emotionally, Carrie and her kinfolk were Alana's extended family. They loved and accepted her, come what may. They were gracious, accepting people who didn't insist of her more than she could willingly give. Except for such moments as those that had just passed with Carrie, they had a live-and-let-live attitude and didn't pester Alana about her reluctance to actively participate in the Christian community.

And for that, Alana was grateful.

She'd believed in a God who cared about her personally, but that had been a long time ago—before her parents' deaths, before she'd gone to live with her aged, widowed grandmother. That was before a lot of bad things had happened to the good people she loved, and she had been convinced that God was not to be trusted. Now she felt that it was wiser to live her life so that with any luck God would forget about her and maybe she could escape the painful, disappointing things that people had assured a crying, flaxen-haired, skinny little girl were "God's will" and not to be questioned.

Alana was so deep in her thoughts, her face haunted as she considered the heartbreak, the hurt, the loss from her past, that she did not hear the front door open. Nor did she detect the stealthy footsteps of a tall, handsome man who approached her. His lower lip momentarily twitched, as if he wasn't sure the smile he bore was quite what he would need to transcend the moment that lay directly ahead.

"Hello. Long time no see, Lana. How've you been?"

The softly drawled words slithered up Alana's spine like cold fingers. Startled, she sprang from the padded chair behind her desk and, with primitive instincts, yanked the sharp letter opener up with her, her blue eyes glittering with frightened fury, radiating a feisty courage that her quaking knees signaled to her she did not really feel. Her heart galloped as she thought of the ominous calls, the notes. Perhaps it wasn't teenagers after all, but a stalker—a psychotic—who'd selected her as the focus of his attention for some insane reason.

Rattled, Alana stared at the man, and with an amateur theater actress's talent, determined to look as brazen and fearless as she could manage. She wanted to kick herself for having unlocked the front door for early morning browsers.

"Who are you? What do you want?" she asked the stranger in a chilly, tough-as-nails tone.

"Goodness! You really don't place me, do you?"

"No," Alana admitted, and squinted up at the man

before she caught herself. She quickly changed her look to an imperious stare that she hoped would leave no doubts about her ability to defend herself. There was something hauntingly familiar about the man's voice, but his face was that of a perfect stranger.

His voiceprint riffled through the file of memories she'd locked away for so long. When the connection was made and she recalled the way a man bearing a voice of the same tone and timbre, but a face so very different, had once lazily caressed her cheek with his fingertips, making her feel so safe, so committed, she gasped in alarm.

No! It could not be Bill!

At the thought, Alana grew flushed, but then she chilled with anger as she remembered the heartache she'd suffered when that man—Bill Sterling—had left her at the altar in the small church in her home town. That fateful day, the wedding guests arrived. The bridegroom did not. Alana had been utterly alone to face them. She no longer had had even Gran to turn to for comfort and solace.

But when she stole another look at the stranger in her store, relief flooded through her. She knew that he was not Bill. The man bore almost no resemblance to Bill aside from his voice and basic size.

"No, I'm afraid I don't place you," Alana said in a cool, indifferent, but very controlled tone. "We see many customers in here each day, and—"

The man's lips quirked into a sardonic grin. "Wrong

frame of reference, Lan." The handsome stranger gave her an almost rakish grin that made her pulse quicken, and he edged closer. "I'm wounded that you don't remember me. But, come to think of it, I shouldn't be surprised. After all, I've had extensive cosmetic surgery after an almost fatal accident. Sort of silly of me to forget that little tidbit. But believe me, I've never forgotten you, Pet."

Pet!

The endearment that had been Bill's way of occasionally addressing her. He'd teasingly called her Pet because he knew that she, who was not about to subject herself to any man, despised the endearment if used by any other person. She had only allowed it from him because she had understood how very much he loved her.

Realization burned a fiery path to her very soul.

So many things were different, but three things remained the same: the shade of his eyes, the color of his hair, and his uncanny ability to wring some kind of response from her with a smile, a word, or a mere glance.

"Bill," she breathed, dazed.

It wasn't a statement. It wasn't a question. But somehow the mere utterance of his name said everything that had been unsaid in the two years since the day she had last not seen him, their wedding day.

"Oh...Bill!"

Alana's eyes filled with tears of joy at seeing him alive, but then the quick emotions evolved to something else.

Alana was dashed with an icy shock that gave way to scalding fury and became tears of anger.

Before Alana could say more than his name, a secretary from an office building nearby slipped in to flick through garments on the sale rack.

Sighing, confused, Alana felt she was drowning in a whirling eddy of unsaid words. Impatiently, angrily, she switched on the store's stereo system and Muzak filled the exquisitely decorated boutique, offering a dram of privacy for the confrontation that was coming too late, but was totally unavoidable if she were ever to live in peace again.

"Well?" Bill prompted, causing Alana to clamp her lips against vitriolic words that wouldn't be fitting for a customer to overhear and would probably cause Carrie, if she were to walk in and witness the scene, to pass out cold.

Piqued, upset, Alana jerked around, slamming a filing drawer shut in a visible display of irritation. Then she as abruptly yanked it open again, grateful for its support. Her legs seemed unwilling to carry both her and the sudden burden of Bill walking back into her life.

"Well?" Bill murmured again. Then his surgically reshaped lips twinkled into a slightly lopsided grin, one that had always struck a chord in Alana, producing some grand effect, whether it was the desire to smack his face in anger, or kiss his lips with her own.

But that was before he'd jilted her without a word of explanation—taking the coward's way out.

When Bill's grin deepened, Alana realized that he was well aware of the effect his presence was having on her and that he seemed to draw relief and encouragement from that fact.

"You're really lookin' good, Lan. Just as good—"

"As good as when you left me at the altar?" She cut in and her eyes flashed. Painful memories overwhelmed her, the way they always did when a golden oldie on the radio or some simple act or event that she'd always associated with Bill triggered a reaction.

"I'm so sorry, Alana. I was such a fool. Such a worldly, thoughtless, heartless, selfish fool," Bill admitted in a low, contrite tone.

Alana gave a scornful laugh. What an actor he was. His performance, expression, demeanor, and delivery were such that she'd almost believed his remorse was sincere.

"Alas, I was an even bigger one!" she retorted.

"I *am* sorry, Lana. Terribly sorry. I don't know if there's any way to make it up to you. Words seem woefully inadequate."

Alana felt as if she shriveled within, but she found it impossible to try to act as if she could gracefully accept his apology. Maybe Carrie could do something like that, but Alana knew that she didn't have it within her. Anger, hate, and revenge were what had given her the strength to endure. She'd lived on not because of anything, but in spite of it. She'd never fantasized that Bill would return.

Never bothered to dream that he'd come to her with tender apologies. She couldn't imagine herself forgiving him because as far as she was concerned, what he'd done to her was unforgivable.

Alana considered what Bill had just said and decided to remark instead of reply. She gave him a cool, wry smile.

"I should have seen it coming, Bill, right?"

His eyes grew distant as his thoughts were forced back to those times. As if it physically pained him, he gave a sad, almost imperceptible nod. "Yes. Probably."

Alana's eyes filled with sudden tears.

"Why didn't you tell me you were going away? Instead of leaving me a laughingstock?" she asked and had to mime her hurt and anger as she shot the secretary at the sale rack surreptitious glances.

"I didn't have time," Bill answered, seeming to measure his words, as if comparing them to a strict code of conduct.

Alana gave him a look of unvarnished disbelief.

"Sure, Bill, sure. And how long had you been planning your great escape? Days? Weeks? Months?"

The gentleness that she'd seen in his eyes was shaken off, replaced by a haunted look of desperation, and Bill gripped her arm as if to make her listen. She shook his touch away, but it was too late. He'd released her of his own volition, and that serenity she'd noticed had returned.

"I didn't have time. I got a call telling me that I was needed—how much I was needed—and I left without taking time to put my personal affairs in order."

"Well your cold feet certainly made a hot trail when you left. You disappeared so fast that your landlord had to call me to ask me what to do with your junk."

Bill's gaze evaded hers.

"I figured he might. And that you could handle it. I knew I could count on you, Alana."

"The way I was unaware that I could not count on you."

"Touché."

Her tone grew airy.

"You skipped out on your landlord the way you skipped out on me."

"He was paid in full. And got to keep the deposit."

"Ah, was I, too, Bill?" Lana's devastated whisper cracked off to become a harsh sob. She stared at him, her eyes beseeching, the stare unbroken as her tears pooled, then spilled over. Lone drops burned a path down her carefully powdered cheeks.

"I gave you my heart, my love, my trust, and I got to keep the ring. Did you consider that payment in full for giving you the privilege of making a fool out of me and for the hours spent sorting out the inconvenience that your mysterious disappearance caused others?"

Bill paled at the accusations.

"Everything you said holds some truth. I...I guess I have this tongue-lashing coming. Maybe you'll never understand the depth of my regret, Alana. I am truly sorry."

"Well, me, too!" she said, gathering control again, as she whisked a tissue from the box on her desk and carefully dabbed at her face and blew her nose. "I'm sorry that I didn't see what was in your head when I thought I knew what was in your heart."

"I didn't even know what was in my heart then, Alana, or what should have been in my heart. I was as much a puzzle to myself as I'm sure I was to you. But now I can explain."

"Oh, no need to at this late date! In your apartment I found it all. I figured it out long ago. But the book that really got my attention—and my goat—was the well worn copy of *How to Disappear*."

Bill gave Alana a sickly groan, but he offered no defense.

"If you didn't want to marry me, you could have told me. I thought you were man enough to be honest with me. I never dreamed you'd take the coward's way out," Alana rushed through her declarations in a grief-torn, high-pitched whisper.

Bill's eyes were as anguished as hers. He started to reach out to her in a gesture of compassionate consolation, but she shrank away from him.

"It must have been awful," he whispered. The look on his face was as if her pain was suddenly his to bear.

"Awful?" Alana cried in a barely discernable whisper. "You underestimate! My great uncle flew up for the wedding, as did his son. My cousin, Kirk, took leave from the armed forces to attend, too, for as you remember, he was going to give the bride away. He was so furious I think he could have killed you with his bare hands. And my mother and father? Probably a mercy they're dead. That day they no doubt turned in their graves, and Gran, too, for she had loved you like a son when we were next door neighbors during high school, Bill."

"I know that Gran loved me," Bill acknowledged quietly.

"And I?" Alana cried the pained question. Her voice became a husky, hoarse murmur. "I hated you, Bill Sterling, more than I'd have believed I could ever despise another human being."

Bill thought it over for a moment, then shrugged and faced Alana with a resolute expression.

"Then I would imagine that perhaps I have cause to be at least a little bit optimistic about us, Pet," he said, and gave her a shaky smile. "For to hate to that extent is certain proof that one has first loved. I regret that I put you through such a travesty. But it's not what you think. I swear it's not."

It was as if Alana had not even heard him.

"You were different that week," she mused. "With time—two years—to sharpen the focus, I later realized just how distant you'd been. Introspective. You acted like you wanted to tell me something but couldn't bear to. You were so preoccupied, even during our tender, romantic moments together. On the other hand, there was a fierce desperation in your goodbye kisses, as if you feared each time would be the last. Yet you were so secretive, as if I were your sworn enemy. A woman not to be trusted."

"Be that as it may seem, Alana, I didn't feel that way. I was simply torn between two choices. Both appealing, but for different reasons."

"Later on," Alana continued her reminiscences, "I remembered all the calls you took, only to deflect them until I was gone. No doubt you returned them the instant I'd departed. I figured it out long ago, Bill. And it hurt to realize why you left. But telling me the truth would have hurt far less than forcing me to hold up my head and live a lie."

"I never meant to hurt you, Lana. And on an immature level of logic I rationalized that I made the choice that I did for us."

"For us?" Alana repeated, giving a bitter laugh.

He nodded. "Yes. For us. Try to believe that."

"I'm imaginative, but I do have my limitations, Bill. Sorry."

"It appears that we really need to talk this through."

"I don't think we have anything left to say. Why bother at this late date? What difference does it make now?"

"It makes all the difference in the world to me. It's important that you hear me out. Forgive me."

"Okay. If you insist," Alana said, and sighed, hoping that if she did his bidding, he would exit her life again and leave her in peace. A better peace, this time, because at least she would know that he was alive and well.

"Tell me: Who was she? And has she now jilted you the way you did me? Is that why you're bouncing back to me?"

Alana asked the questions, wanting the truth. She knew that it could be no more painful than the lie she had lived for two years, trying to salve her battered ego by telling herself that Bill hadn't simply fallen out of love with her. He had had a reason—and a good reason—for leaving.

Bill looked genuinely amazed.

"Woman? There was no other woman."

Alana gave him an arch look.

"If I believed that, Bill, I'd be a prime candidate to acquire bridge property in Brooklyn. Or purchase retirement acreage in the swamplands of Florida."

Bill gave a weary shrug.

"Believe it or not, there was no other woman, Pet."

Alana bristled. "Don't call me 'Pet'!"

"No doubt you've called me a lot worse."

Alana gave an acknowledging laugh, more like a snort.

"I probably have, and with very good reason. And before I cast unpleasant allegations about your general lineage, why don't you do us both a favor and leave? Disappear, Bill, like you did two years ago."

"I'll leave. But not until I have a chance to explain."

"I don't want to hear it."

"Maybe I have a compelling urge to tell you all the things that I wouldn't—*couldn't*—two years ago."

"Save your breath."

"Not if by using it I can save our love. Get things back like they were so that we—"

"Our? We?" Alana managed an expression of amazement. "What's with the *we* bit? Have you a mouse in your pocket?"

"Don't be difficult, Alana."

"Don't be a cad, Bill! You played that role before. And don't return for an encore, ready to portray the contrite lover. I can't take any more of your chameleon disguises or your rave-review acting abilities."

"I don't want to ever again use those talents except under the guidance of a talented director. Now, whether you believe it or not, there was no other woman. Ever."

"Really?" Alana mocked, with wide-eyed innocence. "There was no other woman? Do tell me more," she invited, and dropped into the chair behind her desk, certain that when he gave his explanation, she had better be sitting down.

two

Bill positioned himself behind Alana, gently moved her long hair away from her shoulders, and began kneading the knots of tension from her muscles at the nape of her neck, causing stress to flow away as his soft words of explanation flooded forth.

"There was never another woman, my darling, but there was another country."

Alana craned around to look up at him. Her eyes narrowed, and her pulse quickened as she realized that she was still as attracted to him as she had been when she had so proudly worn his ring. But she hardened her heart against those sentimental, nostalgic feelings.

"Really? What country?" she inquired in a baiting, disbelieving voice.

Bill playfully chucked her chin.

"I wouldn't give you a list of my old loves, Pet, if I were a womanizing man, which I am not. And to keep your pretty head safely empty of details you'd be happier and healthier not knowing, I'll also not reveal the names of countries and regimes with which I've had some...ummm...rather interesting affairs."

Suddenly, it made excruciating, irrevocable sense. Even so, Alana stared at Bill, aghast, when she realized the ramifications. It was the one consideration she hadn't bothered to explore, and it contained the rhyme and reason behind his abandoning her at the altar without leaving any clue to his whereabouts.

There had been one area of Bill's life that Alana had never discussed with him. Several years younger than Bill, she simply hadn't been part of that existence. He had been living in the real world, and she had been habituating the insular world of high school classes, ball games, slumber parties, and church youth group activities. She knew none of the people involved and wasn't sure she would have been bold enough to seek answers from them even if she had.

"Bill, you didn't," Alana breathed denial, even as in her heart she knew it was true.

Bill was resigned. "I'm afraid I most certainly did."

"Why?"

He shrugged, then gave a helpless gesture. "You know the story. I told you how men on a Special Forces A-Team are trained. The knowledge hard won by a Green Beret never leaves. There are always those willing to pay for the expertise of a combatant who may have left the United States armed forces but isn't opposed to accepting a position as a mercenary—a hired gun, if you will. The work is done for our nation or another country, depending

on who offers the right price. In exchange, the buyer gets
fidelity and a willingness to risk one's life for rich men's
political interests in distant, little-heard-of points around
the globe."

"A soldier of fortune!" Alana muttered the dreaded
label.

"The revolutionaries made me an offer that I couldn't
refuse," Bill said.

Alana's lip quivered. Her staring eyes filled with tears.

"*I* made you an offer," she reminded in a bleak whisper.

Bill took her hand and squeezed it, not allowing Alana
to withdraw her fingers when she attempted to.

"And I wish now that I'd taken you up on it. But they
offered me a lot of money, Alana, more money than most
people see in a lifetime. Money that could have financed
our security for a long time if it were invested wisely.
Money that would have supported us, and supported us
well, while allowing me—us—to pursue an acting career.
We wouldn't have had to live an impoverished existence,
and I wouldn't have experienced the sting of shame in
knowing that my wife was supporting me, the struggling
actor.

"I was told it wouldn't be for long—that I'd be helping
my own country. Foreign nations have their own equiva-
lents to the CIA. I was willing to be a hired gun, a soldier
of fortune, a mercenary, yes, but the bottom line is, I would
never fight against what I believed in: freedom!"

Bill's logic, attitude, and motivation provoked an outraged yowl from Lana, and she was glad that Susie, the secretary, had exited the store, tossing a promise over her shoulder to return for a garment on her lunch hour.

"How mercenary!" Alana gasped.

"Undeniably so. I made a mistake. It can happen to anyone. A rash moment, wrong decision, and your life is ruined. Then I was living by a different set of values. I figured that every person had a price. You just had to figure out the right commodity when you made your approach. Search out other's weaknesses. That's what I believed.

"But I've been changed, Alana. Now I believe in a different set of principles, I have another code of conduct. I no longer trust in myself—my wits, my strength, my stamina, my training. I trust in the One Who made me. And in the knowledge found by humbling myself, I received the greatest wisdom. Wisdom sufficient for me to know that I turned my back on one of the most precious things in my life—your love.

"Part of me can't regret that I left as I did, Alana, because in doing so, I found myself...and I found the Lord, my personal Savior. But I've never forgotten you, Alana. I've prayed about this moment, prayed to the Lord God about you. Prayed that when I came to you to apologize, we could start fresh. That's what I want, Alana, more than anything, except for my wish that you will rediscover your faith. I want for us—"

Alana leaped to her feet, her eyes blazing.

"I want you to go—" She bit down on her lip, hard, to keep from losing control of her temper. "Get out!" she commanded softly. Turning away from Bill, she sank back into the chair, her shoulders wracking with sobs. She rammed a finger in the air and gestured wildly, as she stabbed in the general direction of the door.

"You walked out on me once, so do it now—before I throw you out."

Bill smiled at the prospect but quietly stood his ground. "I know karate, Pet, although circumstances would have to be extenuating for me to defend myself against a woman attacker."

A glowering Alana gave him a dark stare.

"Two years have gone by. I know karate, too, Bill."

Bill gave a rich laugh and his eyes were softly amused. "I hardly call three lessons before you quit being proficient in the martial arts. But to test your abilities, I'm certainly willing to make some advances."

"H...how did you know that?" a flustered Alana blurted out, wondering what else Bill had unearthed about her, what kind of dossier he—and his cohorts who staffed the sensitive data possessed by governmental agencies—had compiled in his absence.

Bill drew closer, his eyes tender.

Unsure of how to deal with this new Bill who certainly seemed as changed as he claimed himself to be, Alana shrank away.

"Ma...make one move, Bill, and you're—you're—Bill!"

He made the move by taking one careful step forward. Alana backed up to purchase maneuvering room for even amateurish action, and instead won the humiliating reward of clumsily banging into a filing cabinet, jarring it from its moorings.

Grinning, Bill advanced another step.

An instant later Alana was trapped between a rock solid filing cabinet and Bill's rugged form. Tenderly he cupped her face between his palms. Hands that were so gentle, she realized, even as she knew that in the past they had held the force and knowledge necessary to kill.

It had been two years since Alana had been so close to a man, and the pulse at her neck fluttered. She realized it offered visible evidence of her emotional state when Bill brushed his lips across her skin there, and she was helpless not to shiver from the effect.

"Please, Bill, oh, please. Get out of my life. Just leave me alone."

His lips followed a path toward her trembling lips.

"I can't leave you. I won't. Never again," he vowed.

"Why?" Tears sprang to Alana's eyes, and salt tinged her tone. "Why can't you just go away and leave me in peace?"

"Because I love you, and I believe that deep down you still love me. Our love wasn't what it should've been in the past, Alana. But neither were we. When both of us are transformed by the Lord, then what we had once will become a love meant to be—"

Alana heaved a sigh, but drew in her breath just as quickly after discovering that the sighing had only pressed her closer to Bill's broad chest.

"These...plans...you so optimistically discuss are foolish. It won't happen as you wish, because I no longer love you." She folded her arms across her chest. "And, I do happen to have something to say in the matter."

Bill smiled down at her.

"God willing, I'll teach you to love me again," he whispered in tender warning.

Alana tossed her hair back and gave him a defiant stare. "I vow to be a most unwilling pupil. So perhaps you should settle on another student, Bill. Someone without my peculiar mental blocks where a relationship between us is concerned. If, indeed, you're the Christian man you now profess to be, I should think that you'd humbly heed my wishes and obey my request to leave me alone."

"The Lord pursued me, Alana, and so shall I pursue you, when I feel that He would have me do so. I see it as an exciting, very worthwhile challenge, darling. The things we seek, long for, and pray for the most, are the most treasured when we attain them."

That rationale won an angry breath from Alana before equally scalding words found their way from mind to mouth.

"It's over, Bill," Alana said, even as a rebellious part of her woman's heart clung to the heady, romantic hope that Bill had given her, and fanned it anew, against her better judgment. "But before you leave, please do give me your mailing address. Somewhere around my house is your book, *How to Disappear*. It appears you could use a refresher course so you can give it a practical application. I'll mail it to you."

Bill grinned. "In my absence you've become a strong, independent, feisty woman, Lana."

She gave a bitter laugh.

"You deserve the credit. You who shaped and formed me by your actions, an absent Henry Higgins blissfully unaware of his stunning influence." She, too, gave a theatrical shrug, one that she knew would have impressed the director of their amateur productions. "And surveying the creation—you claim she's not to your liking?"

Bill shook his head. "No, I'm not complaining. I simply feel as if I hardly know her. You." When he spoke his voice was thick. "But I want to. And I want you to be reconciled to the Lord, too, Alana. The way I am. The way others have been. He can heal you in a way that I could never manage, even in my best attempts to make amends."

"If you'll excuse me, Bill," Alana said in a tired tone, "I really do have things to do. Good day, Mr. Sterling." Abruptly she turned away.

"God willing, I'll be back. And Lord willing, Alana Denise Charles, I *will* win your love again."

Alana turned her back on him. She pinched her eyes shut. Two years ago she had suffered agony when she realized Bill was gone from her life, knowing that he had left willingly, but the despairing ache was even greater now because she knew how much he wanted to stay, and she was determined to send him away.

Deep down, Alana knew that she wanted Bill to stay and try to make it up to her, to let him make her the center of his universe again. But a rebellious part of her knew that it could never happen like that. Not ever again. Because if he was as committed to the Lord as Carrie McFarlane was, then Alana would never be first in Bill's life again.

Alana Charles promised herself that she would not be second best in love again. She waited for the door to softly close, signaling Bill's departure.

A floorboard creaked. Gentle hands cupped her shoulders. Unbidden, she allowed herself to be pivoted around and into his arms, the place she belonged.

Alana tried to break away, to resist. His lips were at first tentative, then, when she surrendered, triumphant. She was breathless when he released her.

"God willing, that kiss is just the beginning," Bill vowed. "But a new beginning, so that our love is reborn in the same way we are given rebirth through Christ. Then our love will be as we—and the Lord—wish for it to be."

Alana turned away, pinching her eyes against stinging tears.

"That kiss was goodbye, Bill," Alana informed him, choking down tears. "I won't share you, Bill Sterling. Not with another woman. Not with another country. Not even with God."

"Until we meet again—think of me. I'll be praying for you."

Before Alana could order—or plead—that he leave, Bill was gone, and to her dismay, his departure left a void in her heart that she feared no mere human love could fill.

three

Turning to depart, Bill had brushed a kiss across Alana's cheek, all that was exposed to him as she stared at the beige carpet and her hair fell forward to shield her features from his scrutiny. Even without his command, she knew that she would do little else but think of him.

When the plate glass doors swished open a minute later, Alana was afraid that Bill was back. Instead, it was Carrie, and Alana felt a strange mixture of relieved disappointment.

"Whew! That was some early morning customer I saw come out of the store."

"Susie?" Alana asked innocently. "She plans to come back on her lunch hour to pick up a few things."

"No, not Susie!" Carrie corrected in an indignant tone. "Was he shopping for a wife or girlfriend? Looking for something unique, exotic, and trendy?"

"Somehow, I don't think so. He was looking for something, yes, but I doubt he'll find it," Alana said, realizing that she was being cryptic.

"Oh really?"

Carrie went on with chitchat, and as wooden as she felt, Alana was helpless not to be uncharacteristically unresponsive.

"So who *was* that guy, Lana. I know you, and it's written all over your expression that you two had some kind of confrontation. Disgruntled customer? An irate husband complaining about his wife's charge account? A too-persistent salesman?"

"It was a social call, not business-related."

Carrie's mouth dropped open. She gestured toward the street.

"That handsome fellow is someone you know socially? And you've never told me about him? For shame, Lana. He's gorgeous. And here Mark and I have been wracking our brains, trying to set you up with the absolutely perfect guy. I saw the pin on that guy's lapel, so obviously he's a Christian—"

"As far as you're concerned, that neatly covers up all else, doesn't it?" Alana flared.

Carrie looked hurt, and Alana felt a twinge of guilt. But not to the point where she offered an apology.

"Committed Christians make mistakes," Carrie offered in a careful tone. "We're only human. I...I guess, though, that you're right, and I do have a special empathy with other people, even strangers, when I see outward signs that they're committed Christians. I feel as if I know and understand them because we both have accepted the Lord and rely on Him."

"Well, that Christian man's past is rather checkered.

Not what you'd expect from your average churchgoer's history."

"So were some of the men of old who committed their lives to Christ when He walked on earth." Carrie paused, seeming to sense that she had to tread carefully to keep from crossing invisible boundaries she felt Alana had placed all around.

"So, that good looking guy," Carrie continued, "is he an old friend, a long lost relative? From the look on your face, I can tell that in some way he's special to you. Or, at least if he's not special, he has the capacity to provoke some pretty strong emotions within you."

"That he does," Alana sighed. "And I don't appreciate the kinds of feelings he causes within me."

"You're not on the best of terms?"

"You can say that!"

"Ah, but it's all in the past, I see. You're getting along quite well now."

Alana gave her business partner a sharp look.

"What makes you say that?"

"Your lipstick's smeared."

"And your eyesight is unbelievable. And your curiosity too much."

Carrie shrugged. "Your tongue is a bit sharper than usual, too."

"I'm sorry, Carrie. But I'm really hurting. I guess I should consider telling you the truth."

"The truth can set you free," Carrie murmured.

"Another Scripture verse?"

"Yep," Carrie replied. "The usual source of my famous and applicable quotations."

Alana made a face. But then she swiped at a tear, and Carrie crossed the boutique and put her arms around her.

"I'm your friend. You've let me share your joys. Let me share your heartache. The truth isn't to be feared, Alana. It's to be respected, appreciated, and learned from. So, what's the story?"

"That man," Alana said, and her voice grew squeaky with tears as she gestured toward the street where his car had been parked, "once meant the world to me. I loved him enough to want to...to plan to...marry him. Then he left me without the decency to even say goodbye! He left me at the altar—disappeared on what was to be our wedding day."

"Oh, Alana! I had no idea. I'm so sorry. That had to have hurt unlike anything else. The hurt. The rejection. The embarrassment."

"Yes!" Alana said, wiping her eyes as she soundlessly wept.

"You must have hated him."

"I did!" Alana said and realized that she felt oddly relieved with the confession of the ugly emotion. "I did. I have. I...I still do!" she insisted, even as she was not sure she could accurately identify the emotion she felt. Maybe it wasn't hate, but she wasn't ready to label it anything else. She wasn't sure she could, even if she wanted to, for she was reeling with confusing feelings. She needed a swatch of emotions, like a color wheel, to be able to determine an exact match. Only then could she correctly assess the feelings she had blocked out for so long.

"I'm sure that you haven't hated this man any more than he's despised himself for his actions that so grievously injured you," Carrie ventured in a reflective tone as she thought it over.

Alana took a deep breath.

"So he says. But talk is cheap," she pointed out, then steeled herself against the stab of hurt that she knew would slash her to the marrow, and did, when she considered that Bill's remorse might have been a carefully contrived performance. One of the best of his life.

"Actions speak louder than words, sometimes, Alana."

"Not when you're an actor by profession," Alana corrected her friend. "Oh, Carrie. I'm so confused. I don't know who—or what—to believe. Or even what to feel. I'm numb."

"When I can't trust my head, and I don't dare trust my heart, and I certainly don't dare trust my feelings—because they're feelings, not facts—" Carrie confided, "That's when I know that I can trust the Lord. He will guide me safely when my human abilities might lead me incorrectly. So pray about it, Alana. And I will, too, more than I already am. Mark prays on your behalf, too."

That was a strange realization to Alana. She'd never asked for their prayers. She felt a bit piqued thinking that they'd been presumptuous enough to pray for her without her permission. But then she felt a warm glow when she realized that they'd done so, unbidden, because they loved and cared for her enough to want her to be happy and kept safe.

More words from Carrie and thoughts within Alana were cut off by the telephone ringing just as the bell above the door tinkled to signal the arrival of a customer.

"Get the customer," Alana hissed, furtively dabbing at her tear-reddened eyes. "I'm in better shape to field a phone call than handle someone in person."

"Sure thing," Carrie agreed and gave Alana a comforting squeeze on the forearm before she turned away to greet the customer with a cheerful word.

"The Shoestring Boutique, Alana speaking. May I help you?" she answered in a controlled tone that she believed didn't reveal how recently she had been weeping.

"I'm watching you. I know where you are. I always know where you are. I will come for you when the time is right. Until then, remember that I am like God, Alana. I am everywhere. You'll never get away from me. You'll never want to, either—"

"Is this some kind of joke?" Alana said. "If so, it's not at all funny! I've had enough of this, and I'm going to report your calls to the police—"

"Involve the authorities, my darling, and you'll live to regret it. In fact, you might die regretting it."

The line went dead.

Alana was still holding the receiver a moment later when it issued a taped message that her telephone was off the hook, followed by loud blasts that carried across the room. Dazed, she hung up.

"Who was it?" Carrie asked.

"A wrong number, I guess," Alana fibbed. "They hung up as soon as I answered."

Who was it? Alana wondered as her mind cried out for identifying factors so she could recognize her tormentor. The voice was unfamiliar, the inflection difficult to place, and she wasn't sure that the voiceprint even matched the other rare calls when the person who was harassing her did more than breath heavily into the telephone. The silences unnerved her, and the sense of being watched against her will caused gooseflesh to rise on her skin.

A sudden, unnerving idea occurred to her. Obviously Bill had been in town a few days, and that paralleled with the period during which the strange calls and notes had begun arriving. He had done a lot of acting. And, in the espionage and mercenary activities, surely he had been forced to adopt unfamiliar accents in order to successfully disguise himself.

Could he be the person behind the odd, vaguely threatening contacts? Was he so intent on having her that if he couldn't win her back through declarations that he was a changed man, then he was determined to *scare* her back into his arms?

Alana shivered. She'd wanted to trust the Bill she'd met. But part of her warned her not to let down her guard. She didn't know where, or whom, to turn to. Carrie always had the ready answer—the one she gave so frequently that it sometimes risked sounding like a blithe, trite suggestion.

Trust in the Lord, Alana had heard, time and again. But she wasn't ready for that. Not yet.

four

Alana yawned and leaned back in her desk chair as Carrie entered the Shoestring Boutique, the empty bank bag in one hand, the deposit receipt in her other.

"It's been a long day," Alana said.

Carrie waved the deposit slip. "But it was also a good day!"

Alana nodded, then shrugged.

"Good in some ways. Lousy in others. But inarguably it has been long. I'm glad that it's quitting time. My big plans for the night are to walk home, turn off the phone, and soak in a bubble bath. The perfect antidote for a day like this."

"Sounds good," Carrie agreed. "But will you have time?"

Alana shot her a glance.

"Of course I'll have time. Why wouldn't I? I have nothing on the docket except to open the store tomorrow morning, and then get ready for the community theater group tryouts tomorrow night."

Carrie sighed and rolled her eyes expressively as she gestured toward the flyer printed on colorful paper that was taped in the boutique's display window.

"Don't tell me you've forgotten," she chided.

Alana halted midway through retrieving her wrap from the coat tree and wheeled to confront her partner.

"Forgotten what?" Alana asked as the expression on her face gave an indication that she was flicking through a mental appointment book. She gave a soft groan. "Oh, no. Tonight's not the night, is it?"

Carrie nodded. "It certainly is. So you do have plans."

Alana was about to beg off, but she knew that tired, depressed, upset, or not, she simply couldn't do that to her friend. Especially not after the way she had made a special point to ask Carrie to reserve a ticket for her.

Over the past months, Alana had felt herself sliding into a state where she simply wanted to isolate herself and spend her time with a good book, watching television, or doing absolutely nothing, instead of being with other people. She realized that the unhealthy desire could intensify if she allowed it to, so she had taken steps to protect herself from such tendencies.

Since the men's group of Mark Landry's church was sponsoring a church supper followed by a concert presented by Christian performers, Alana had told Carrie to get her a ticket so they could attend together.

"What time are the big doings?" Alana asked lightly, although inside she was feeling resigned and hoping her lack of enthusiasm wasn't apparent in her tone.

"The church hall will be opening around six. But my

contribution to the potluck is a seven-layer salad so I don't have to get there until right before it's time to eat. The concert is at eight. Mark'll probably pick me up around six-thirty. We'll swing by to get you within another five minutes."

"Sounds good, but I can drive if you and Mark don't want to be bothered," Alana said, thinking to herself that then she could escape at the first chance she got to leave without being rude or unfriendly. She wasn't sure she was up to hearing any personal testimonies, either, as individuals eagerly shared how wonderful their lives had become when hers couldn't have been more wretched.

Carrie shrugged. "That's up to you. But did you get your car into the shop yet?"

"Uh-uh. I haven't had time. Well, that's not quite right. You know how it is these days. I have the time but the shop has to work my repair job in. They booked me as far ahead as my doctor does! They pick it up next Tuesday. Until then I really haven't been driving except out of sheer necessity, and then I don't trust the brakes very far."

"Then it's settled, my dear. Until you get the brake line checked, if you're not within walking distance of where you're going, you're going to ride with Mark and me."

"All right," Alana agreed, giving a faint chuckle. "I'll tag along with you two and be odd man out."

"We love your company, dear girl, in case you hadn't noticed. I'll be relieved to have you with us. I know I don't have any desire to drive tonight," Carrie went on in a chatty tone. "Have you heard the forecast?"

"No. Bad?"

Carrie made a face. "Snow showers at best. Freezing rain at worst."

Alana groaned. "Metro-St. Louis's favorite selection from the weather menu."

"Actually, though, Lana, it's been a mild winter," Alana pointed out. "We've been blessed in that department."

"Thank God for that."

"You know, winter's half over," Carrie mused. "And we've got a really solid inventory of ladies' insulated boots. If this turns into a bona fide seasonal storm, I think we should run a special so we improve our cash flow and turn over our inventory of footwear. What do you think? Although it doesn't seem like it, spring is just around the corner, and with it, huge shipments of new fashions. We do need to make room."

"What do I think? That I've got a brilliant business partner. Consider it done. Good idea, Car."

"Great!" Carrie replied. "I thought you'd go for it. We can discuss ad copy somewhere between the pastor blessing the food and his offering the benediction at evening's end."

"Okeydoke. See you later." Alana checked her wristwatch. "If I hurry, I've still got time for a quick bubble bath."

"Enjoy!" Carrie said as Alana secured the top button of her coat and slid on her supple, calfskin gloves.

"See you later!" Alana called out in a cheerful tone that was in direct contrast with how she felt.

There was an unpleasant churning in her stomach—nerves, she knew—and as she stepped into the street, she found herself looking around, sharply so, hoping that her eyes would miss nothing.

The street looked as it generally did at quitting time, but Alana found herself scrutinizing the area a second time, seeking to detect some telling little detail that was out of the ordinary. Something that perhaps only she would notice but that could alert her to danger from which she could attempt to keep herself safe.

"Don't be so paranoid!" she muttered under her breath. It was an act of will, but Alana made herself stop looking around, and she walked the four blocks to her apartment without glancing up except to wait for the stoplights to signal for her to cross the street.

She hoped that she didn't appear tense, in case she was being watched. If her tormenter knew that he or she was really bothering her, Alana feared that it would increase the individual's perverse enjoyment, whereas if she carried on as if nothing was wrong, the perpetrator might decide their strange cat-and-mouse campaign was no fun and focus the unwanted and upsetting attentions on another victim.

Even so, Alana carefully looked around as she let herself into her apartment house and made sure the lobby was secure. She paused a moment to make certain the hallway to her quarters was empty before she stepped from the elevator at the fifth floor.

Once she was in her apartment and had secured the deadbolt behind her, Alana felt safe. Quickly she set about her ordinary routine, flicking on the gas range to heat water for tea. After enjoying a hot drink and a moment to riffle through the mail she had collected from the box in the lobby, she began to brush her hair, then decided to shampoo it in the sink basin as the bath water ran, causing a delicate floral scent to waft outward into the steamy room.

At work, Alana had threatened to turn off the telephone, and when it rang a moment after she'd slid into the depths of the comfortably hot tub, she wished she had.

Alana boosted up, taking a mountain of bubbles with her, and strained to reach the portable telephone she'd placed on the vanity. As she fumbled for the "on" button with damp fingers, she felt a sense of trepidation at answering. Not that many people called her at home, except Carrie, and they had just finalized their plans minutes earlier, Alana realized. Her pulse quickened in alarm when she considered that it could be another one of those calls.

She froze with her finger poised on the button and

considered letting the answering machine in her living room take the call so she could phone the caller after she'd finished her bath, but she realized that if she let terror direct her actions, soon she would be looking over her shoulder in fear, paralyzed to the point of seriously isolating herself—hiding out—as she had done when Bill had disappeared from her life. Alana realized that if she gave in to the various unpleasant sensations and fears and lived her life accordingly, she would have a hand in emotionally crippling herself.

Bill! When Alana thought of his name and remembered how unexpectedly he had reentered her life, unidentifiable feelings ricocheted through her, leaving her unable to decide if his arrival made her feel anguish, excitement, or a strange blend of the two powerful emotions.

Maybe it was Bill who was calling, she thought. And before she could censor the impulsive action, she flicked the button and breathlessly answered, doing it before her head had time to argue with her heart and cause a stalemate that would stymie any action on her part.

"Hi! It's me," Carrie said. "I just wanted to call to let you know that it'll probably be a foursome tonight."

"A what?" Alana asked, feeling herself frown. A chill pervaded her, even though the water was soothingly hot.

"A foursome," Carrie cheerfully repeated. "But not like you're thinking. We're not springing a blind date on you. So don't worry. There are no strings attached. Mark called a while ago. You know he's been running an ad to rent the extra suite in their office complex?"

"I saw the ad last week."

"Well a private investigator who's setting up a new business venture is interested in signing a lease. Ordinarily, Mark would take a colleague out to discuss it over dinner. He asked the guy if it would be okay if they'd talk it over at a church supper, and the fellow doesn't seem to mind.

"Mark really wants to rent the space to this guy. Sometimes Mark's used PIs to do investigations that are beyond his ken or to collect evidence in domestic suits, interview potential witnesses, that kind of thing. He seems to think that with this guy's reputation and ethics, he'd like to have him conveniently in the same complex for his own use and for quick and easy referrals."

"Ummm. Sounds like it could be a mutually beneficial situation."

"That's what Mark says."

"Okay, I don't mind," Alana said. "The more the merrier as long as you realize that he's doing business with Mark, and that it's not someone in whom you're trying to interest me."

"Would I do that?" Carrie asked in a flip tone, then gave a guilty little laugh that seemed to admit that she certainly would. And had. "Anyway, from the look you had on your face this morning shortly after your lipstick was smeared,

I'd say that your heart was already taken by what's-his-name who just walked smack dab into front and center stage of your life. Far be it from me to throw romantic competition directly into the path of a brother in Christ. Maybe with my influence, Mark's example, and a bit of input from what's-his-name, you'll end up one day returning to—"

"I'll be ready right on time," Alana cut in, not wanting to hear what she knew Carrie wanted to say.

"Okay. Sorry that I started to run on. See you then! Tonight's going to be great!"

"I'm sure it will."

As Alana flicked off the portable phone, then gently laid it on the rug beside the tub, she felt the familiar pain in her heart that engulfed her whenever she thought of the love that had once been, and the love that had been lost.

Now Bill said he wanted her back again. Alana didn't know what she wanted. But she knew that she couldn't stop the clock. And she certainly couldn't turn back the hands of time and return to the past to correct errors made then. Bill Sterling had made so many mistakes that Alana considered them nigh on unforgivable.

A short while later, to her surprise, Alana found herself willing to abandon the steaming, sweetly scented bubble bath a few minutes earlier than she'd initially planned. It wasn't until she gave the seemingly impulsive action a bit of conscious thought that she realized she had been motivated to cut short her bubble bath in order to extend the amount of time she had planned on for dressing. Deep down she admitted to herself that she desired to have more time to spend doing her hair and makeup and coordinating her outfit so that she would look as attractive as possible when she was introduced to Mark's new business associate.

Alana had once heard it said that the best way to forget an old love was to find a new love. Until that night, she hadn't really been looking. But now she was, for with Bill's return to her life, he'd brought a host of conflicting memories that she suddenly found impossible to suppress.

Alana gazed into her beautifully made-up eyes as she inserted the mascara applicator brush into the tube and smiled at her reflection. Impulsively she reached for the vial containing her best perfume and dabbed the exotic scent at her pulse points, at the base of her throat, and behind her ears.

Because of her relationship with Carrie, over time Alana had come to know Mark Landry well, and she respected and admired him, considering Carrie a fortunate woman to have a fiancé as handsome, successful, ethical, decent, and loving as Mark. In fact, a few times Alana had wistfully teased Carrie that she should get Mark cloned and make a host of other women as happy as she was.

At the thought, Alana realized that she felt a surge of anticipation, for she knew that if Mark Landry was impressed enough with his prospective lessee to invite him to talk business at a church social, than the town's newest PI might be the kind of person Alana would find worthwhile to get to know.

During the past twelve months, Carrie and Mark had submitted any number of eligible bachelors to Alana's attention, but she hadn't really been interested. She simply couldn't open up to a new relationship, for she felt that she could never trust to the degree that a man might one day ask her to.

But now that she'd encountered Bill Sterling again, her heart seemed to have been reactivated and a void begged to be filled. For that, she wanted almost any man other than the betrayer from the past who now wanted—prayed—to be the one to give meaning to her life.

All day long Alana had found herself spiraled back in time. Instead of concentrating on the present moment, she'd been trapped in a period several years past. Before Alana's eyes had swirled a kaleidoscope of places she and Bill had gone, things they had done, friends they had enjoyed, the love they had shared.

"The best way to forget an old love is to find a new love," Alana whispered again, reinforcing her resolve after she traced on lipstick, then blotted her mouth and studied the effect.

And at that moment she made up her mind that unless Mark's new lessee was an absolute toad, she would hope that he'd be a prince for the night. A prince with the possibility for developing a new, maybe even a permanent and enduring, relationship. Hopefully a relationship that could forever drive from her mind and heart the intense feelings that Bill Sterling had stirred up within her heart, causing chaos and confusion to reign.

five

Alana was dressed and ready to go at six-thirty. As good as her word, Carrie buzzed from the lobby five minutes later.

Alana felt a stab of disappointment that a trio didn't await her as she stepped from the elevator. Alana realized that Carrie correctly translated the expression on her face when she explained, "Mark and his friend are circling the block. There were no close parking spaces available. They'll pick us up when they make another lap. Ready to go?"

"As ready as I'll ever be," Alana said, as she fell in step with her friend and exited to the city sidewalk.

"Great!" Carrie murmured.

As they waited for Mark's car to come around the corner and reappear, Alana realized that she was dying with curiosity, and she was disappointed that her business partner hadn't at least offered a general impression of Mark's prospective lessee.

Alana wondered if it were possible that she could broach the subject without making Carrie aware that, contrary to what she'd said during her bubble bath, she was interested in her evening's companion. When Carrie said nothing,

Alana decided that she couldn't easily bring up the topic and concluded that an air of disinterest probably served her best.

Alana was shivering as she waited curbside next to Carrie while Mark braked to a halt. With agile movements, he hopped out to help the women into his car. Mark tucked Carrie into the front seat, then opened the rear door to help Alana into the back.

"I'll make introductions!" Carrie gaily offered, swiveling around as she secured her seatbelt. Her eyes were sparkling as if she could scarcely contain a precious secret.

Alana, who had leaned forward, ducking to get into the medium-sized sedan, came face to face with the eyes of the gentleman who had leaned across to assist her.

Their eyes met—then clashed.

Alana felt the color drain from her face as her knees went weak a split second before her heart escalated to a jack-hammer cadence.

Bill Sterling!

Carrie's voice was a satisfied purr. "Alana, meet Bill Sterling. Bill, Alana Charles."

Alana swallowed hard and found speech impossible.

Bill grinned, ducking his head as if in a mock bow. His smile was pleasant but triumphant, riling Alana's temper.

"A pleasure, Miss Charles," he said, and formally extended his hand to her.

"I was delighted to be able to spend an evening with my

friend, Carrie," Alana replied in an even tone, but her eyes flashed a warning.

Mark, who was unaware that the pair knew each other, seemed to believe nothing was amiss. For her part, Carrie looked like the cat that had swallowed the canary.

Bill, with his hand still extended, cleared his throat as if to prompt Alana into action. She gave an aloof glance and proffered a polite handshake.

Alana had expected Bill to squeeze her hand in bland greeting, then release her and make benign conversation with Mark and Carrie. Instead, Alana was both upset and elated to discover that Bill refused to release her hand. Knowing that she wouldn't make a scene, he seemed to enjoy the moment immensely. He continued to hold her hand until they arrived at the church meeting hall. When Bill surrendered her hand, Alana was both relieved and dismayed by the conflicting emotions flooding through her.

"Come with me, Alana. We can check in with the ladies in the kitchen to see if they need our help." Carrie made a shooing gesture with her hand. "You men run along and entertain yourselves. Save Alana and me seats at whatever table you choose!"

During the car ride, Alana had wished to be anywhere but in Bill Sterling's presence, but once Carrie had wrested her from his side, Alana was overcome by a strange longing that she neither understood nor appreciated.

What she liked even less was the prickle of jealousy that rippled through her when, from the corner of her eye, she saw Mark introducing Bill to his friends.

Although Alana had tried to reassure herself that she had no interest whatsoever in her former fiancé, she was all too aware that there were a number of well-dressed, attractive women who looked as if they would be delighted to keep the company of Mr. Bill Sterling, PI.

"What's wrong with you?" Carrie inquired, giving Alana a studied look. "Headache?"

"Something like that," Alana said.

Carrie gave her a more assessing look. "Ah. I think it's more aptly termed a heartache."

Alana's lower lip trembled. She blinked quickly to ward off a stinging deluge of tears. "And I think that you, my dear, are treading on extremely thin ice."

"I don't mean to meddle or intrude, Alana. But Bill seems so nice. Mark thinks so, too. It seems incredible that he could ever hurt someone. Especially you. Lannie, I've seen how Bill Sterling looks at you. The man loves you. Give him a chance."

"Never!" Alana said, her tear-filmed eyes flashing.

Carrie pulled her friend into a private alcove. "I know that you want to, Alana. I can read you like a book. You're still in love with him."

"I am not!" she protested. Then, in the face of Carrie's wry look, she reiterated, "And even if I were, it'd do no good. I don't want anything to do with him. Ever."

"Why?" Carrie asked, persisting.

"Why? I'll tell you why! Because what he did to me was totally without conscience."

"That may have been the old Bill Sterling. The new one is a different man. He's a man you can trust."

"I have no desire to try."

"You won't give him a chance? He's been an adoring, smitten gentlemen every moment he's been with you. It's obvious that the man cherishes you. There are many women who'd have thought they'd died and gone to heaven to have such a fine, hardworking, successful Christian man looking at them the way he looks at you."

"Then these fine...Christian...women are welcome to such a fine...Christian...man. I don't want him."

"You can fib about that to me," Carrie said. "But you can't lie to yourself. Give the guy a chance."

"He had his chance. He messed up."

"Oh, Lannie, we all mess up. No one is perfect, except for Jesus, Who came down from heaven to show us how to live. Think of where we'd be if the Lord refused to forgive our mistakes."

"I don't want to think about it," Alana blurted out.

Carrie gave her a tender look and patted her hand. "I know you don't. Many people feel as you do. But it's only because Mark, Bill, and I love you that we want you to concern yourself with eternity and returning to fellowship with God rather than living for the moment."

"Do we have to discuss this?"

"No," Carrie said, giving a sudden grin. "It seems that perhaps I've said too much." Her grin deepened. "Forgive me?" she asked, with a twinkle in her eyes.

Alana gave a faltering smile in return. "Of course. I can't stay mad at you."

"Try not staying angry with Bill Sterling, either," Carrie suggested, but in a voice so soft that Alana wasn't sure if the thought had fallen from her friend's lips or emanated from a wellspring in her conscience that seemed to cling to the philosophies that Carrie sometimes shared.

"They're about to start serving," Mark said, as he and Bill approached Alana and Carrie and prepared to escort them to their table.

"Men on one side, women on the other," Carrie declared.

Alana felt relief. At least she wouldn't be seated right beside Bill. But a moment later, she was wishing that she had been seated beside him. Then he would have had to crane around to keep his eyes on her. As it was, she was unnerved by the way Bill's attention was riveted on her. Alana hardly tasted the food that Mark, Bill, and Carrie remarked was delectable.

She was relieved when Carrie suggested that they help the church women with cleanup chores in the kitchen. The time sped by all too quickly, and then she was forced into

Bill's company again as they took their seats and settled in for the beginning of the concert.

Alana wasn't certain exactly about what she'd expected. The way the evening had seemed to be on a downward spiral every moment since she'd first locked stares with Bill Sterling, she was surprised to discover that the sacred music caused her to feel uplifted. To her amazement, she was feeling oddly happy. Serene. At peace. Almost forgiving.

"Wasn't it a wonderful concert?" Carrie mused as they walked through the chilly night air to the car that Mark had already warmed up for the quick trip home.

"Inspiring," Bill said.

"Very nice," Alana agreed.

Bill paused. "We should all do something like this again."

"I'd like that," Carrie said. "Mark would, too."

Count me out! Alana thought, but when she said nothing, she caught Bill and Carrie exchanging glances. She could almost read their minds thinking, *Progress, not perfection.*

Mark, Bill, and Carrie chatted away so that Alana wasn't called upon to say anything on the brief ride to her apartment building.

"You can let me out in front of my building," Alana said.

"Does your building have a doorman?" Bill asked.

"Of course not," Alana said. "It's hardly the Ritz."

"In that case, if Mark doesn't mind circling the block a time or two, I'd like to see you safely to your door."

"There's no need," Alana said, even as his cautious attitude suddenly made her remember what, at least for a few hours, she'd managed to forget: she might be in danger.

Bill shrugged. "Perhaps there's no need, but I'd like to make sure that you get in safely."

"I've been seeing to my own needs for two years. I'm a big girl now, Bill. I don't need you—or anyone."

"That's where you're wrong. I agree with you, Pet. Perhaps you don't need me, but you do need Someone who loves you even more than I. Alana, I love you so much that I would die for you. But you know how much Jesus loves you and that He already died for you."

"Bill...please," Alana whispered in anguish, begging him to leave her in peace.

"We'll only be a moment, Mark," Bill said.

Before Alana could protest further, Bill ushered her into the lobby and up to the fifth floor. She was afraid that he would try to kiss her good night at her door, but when he didn't, she was disappointed.

"Stay sweet," he whispered. "See you around."

Alana had expected Bill to make arrangements to see her again. When he did not, again, she found herself disappointed.

"Good night, Bill," she said.

"Good night, Alana. And goodbye."

Suddenly, the tables were turned. Bill's words seemed to contain meanings on several levels, and as Alana realized that there might be a finality to his "good-bye," irrational as it was, she found herself wanting to see him again.

Maybe he'd finally gotten the message, Alana tried to convince herself a half hour later, but the thought gave her no comfort. And the thought that followed it made her eyes widen in alarm. For maybe, just maybe, Bill had met someone that evening who he found more attractive than he did Alana.

At that moment Alana realized how much she still loved Bill Sterling. And an instant after that, the telephone rang.

Thinking of Bill, Alana rushed to answer.

six

The next morning when the radio alarm shrilled, Alana groaned, rolled over, and groggily slapped at the radio, attempting to find the button that would silence the grating buzzer.

Her eyes were caked with grit, and her aching head felt thick and heavy. She cracked one eye open and realized that she'd only managed to fall asleep two hours earlier and then only due to sheer exhaustion.

She considered calling the local police precinct, but as she began to imagine what a conversation with an interviewing officer would be like, she realized that there was a good chance she would appear flighty, paranoid, and hysterical. She found it all too easy to believe that she would not be taken seriously.

But she was so unnerved on her walk to the Shoestring Boutique that by the time she arrived—to open early—she had mustered the wherewithal to dial the police station. To her relief the officer at the desk was pleasant. That encouraged her to continue on. Soon, however, the conversation disintegrated exactly as she had anticipated.

"I can appreciate your concern, ma'am," the officer said in a polite tone. "It sounds like a matter that is best investigated by the telephone company. They have the equipment to catch the perpetrator. We can't do anything without their cooperation. Your best option is to call someone at your company's business office and discuss the matter with them."

Before she could lose her resolve, Alana checked her telephone directory and placed a quick call. A velvet-voiced woman answered and listened patiently as Alana explained her dilemma.

"Most crank calls are just that—pranksters having fun at another's expense," the woman assured. "Most crank callers are actually harmless people. Granted, they are sick individuals, but they usually are harmless. You're probably not in physical danger," the woman comforted.

"But what can I do?" Alana cried, frustrated, her voice cracking. She drew a deep, ragged breath. "What can your company do?"

"We do have steps we take," the woman said. "Please give me your name and address and I'll send you the appropriate paperwork to fill out. Take it to the sheriff for your county, get him to sign it, and have him return it to our address. As soon as we receive the documents, we'll install a monitoring device on your line."

Helplessly Alana looked at the calendar. "But that will take days!" she protested.

Alana could sense the woman shrugging, even though not another word was said.

"Thank you for your time," Alana said, aware that her voice had grown cold. "But somehow it doesn't seem worth the trouble."

"If you have further problems, please do contact us. I'll be glad to drop the paperwork into the mail—or you can drive to our office complex and pick up the documents, pay a personal call on the sheriff, and have a deputy deliver the completed paperwork to our attention. That could speed up the process a bit."

Alana thought of her impaired brakes. She considered having to take time away from the store and the need to make necessary explanations to Carrie.

"Forget it," Alana said, her tone bleak. "It really doesn't seem worth the trouble. Perhaps whoever is harassing me will grow tired of it, leave me alone, and either dispense with such foolishness altogether or focus on some other unlucky individual."

"It's up to you," the company employee responded. "If you have further problems, don't hesitate to contact us."

Alana hung up. She wished she could have slammed down the receiver, but she knew that the telephone employee was only doing her job, just as had been the desk sergeant at the precinct station.

Alana recognized the limitations brought on by the high-tech age of computers and state-of-the-art surveillance equipment. Phone companies and police departments couldn't move in like a SWAT team because of one person's over-the-phone allegation. Sick individuals might make false accusations and set authorities on innocent people as a form of harassment. In other cases, a person might report a fictitious incident just to attract some exciting attention.

Alana was relieved when customers began to flock into her shop, making her too busy to think about the threatening messages. She was glad that her evening would be fully occupied at the community theater where she would be trying out for a role in the local production of *Oklahoma!*

She hoped that if she made it difficult or impossible for the person who was harassing her to make personal contact, then her tormenter might become frustrated enough to search for a more available subject.

There was a lull in the flow of customers, and Alana was enjoying a momentary respite. She'd just poured herself a cup of coffee and was seated at her desk, about to go over some invoices, when the bell above the door tinkled to signal that someone had entered the shop.

Ever since Bill had walked in the day before, Alana's heart had skipped a beat whenever the bell sounded, and she realized that she was hoping for Bill's return. Each time she would look up with anticipation, but her hopes had been dashed as someone other than Bill had made an entrance.

This time the individual wore a gray courier's uniform. Alana frowned, perplexed, because she couldn't recall any other time when a courier had made a delivery at her business. She thought that the man might be taking a break from his job to check out the store's offerings for a possible gift for a wife or girlfriend. But when the man looked around, then came directly toward her, she realized he was there to deliver something.

"Alana Charles? That you?" he asked in a brusque tone.

"Yes."

"Okeydoke, ma'am. These are for you!" With a flourish and an apologetic smile, the courier produced a bouquet of dead flowers tied with an elaborate black ribbon from which a florist's card hung by a silver thread.

"What on earth?" Alana gasped in astonishment.

"We only deliver," the courier said in an abashed tone.

"But do you—"

"Have a nice day, Miss!" the courier said and quickly exited the store.

Alana stared at the dead, dry, prickly bouquet that had been shoved into her hands. She reached for the discreet card.

With trembling fingers she opened it. Written in neat cursive were the words, "Break a leg, my darling."

Alana stared at the message and the disgusting bouquet and fought down sobs that threatened to erupt.

Stunned, she flipped over the small envelope that contained the card, and her heart lifted when she saw that there was a florist's imprint stamped on it. Quickly she consulted the local directory and dialed.

"Hi. My name is Alana Charles, and I would like to talk to someone about a bouquet of awful looking old flowers that I received—"

"We do our best to create lovely and long-lasting floral pieces," the woman said in a crisp tone. "Perhaps you stored the bouquet too close to a source of heat. Or forgot to check water levels. Sometimes a bit of aspirin in the water extends the life of cut flowers—"

"I just received the bouquet. The flowers are dead!" Alana interrupted.

"Dead?"

"Yes, dead!" Alana repeated.

"Then I assure you, Miss, you did not receive them from our establishment. We have a store policy not to send out dead flowers to anyone, for any price."

"But attached to the flowers was an envelope with your store's address imprinted on the back—"

"We have an area in the store where a goodly selection of gift cards to fit all occasions are kept with a writing desk. We haven't taken any security measures to prevent persons walking into our store from purloining our card stock," the woman explained. "I can appreciate how distraught you are, ma'am, and that's exactly why our store has a policy against sending dead flowers as a joke or an insult."

"If...if I were someone who wanted to send someone this

kind of...joke...then there are florists in the area who'd do it?"

"Well...yes," the woman admitted, and there seemed to be great reluctance in her tone to even discuss the matter.

"Please, I'm desperate," Alana said. "Someone is bothering me. I've had crank calls, messages, and now this. I don't know if I'm in danger or what. I've called the police, but they feel they can't get involved with such insubstantial evidence. Could you please just give me the names of the florists who will send dead flowers so I can talk to them?"

"Well...I don't know," the woman said, and Alana was fearful that the employee might hang up.

"Please? It could be a matter of life or death," Alana said, realizing that she could sound melodramatic. But when her voice helplessly cracked with tears and emotions, the woman sighed and relented.

She provided the names of two area shops. "Some people will do anything for money," she added critically. "I hope you will keep that in mind if there are flower orders in your future. Ethics are an important part of our business."

"Thanks," Alana said, feeling relieved. "And as helpful as you've been, you can count on me for future business."

As she hung up, Alana found herself hoping that the flower shop wouldn't get a lot of business on her behalf—from friends ordering funeral sprays for her burial. With that thought and her increasing sense of desperation, Alana reached for the telephone directory again.

The first flower shop the sales clerk had named stated that due to the unpopularity of dead flowers with the recipients, they no longer provided such bouquets.

"It wasn't worth it," the man said, his voice warm and friendly. "When we started doing it by popular request, we thought it was just a gag. But we soon realized how affronted the recipients were. We want flowers to signify happiness. So providing dead flowers is a service we choose to no longer offer."

"Then I thank you for the information—and I also thank you for making a sane business decision," Alana said.

With trepidation, she dialed the remaining number.

"Yeah, the flowers came from this shop," a man said. "The bouquet was dead, but the guy's money was plenty green. He bought the bouquet and took possession of it. We used to deliver dead flowers, but our van drivers didn't like the static they got from people receiving them. Now we have a policy that we'll sell dead floral material, but we don't deliver. If someone wants to buy it, they can. What they do with it is their business, but we don't want to be involved on a personal level."

"I'm sure you don't," Alana said. "It's a devastating experience. So you don't use a courier to deliver?"

"Nope!" the man said. "If a courier brought your bouquet, then whoever bought the flowers from us arranged for that."

Alana's heart suddenly lifted. "Do you remember the person who came in and got a bouquet of dead flowers? The one you fixed for me?"

"Well, yeah, he was just a regular Joe. Someone you could see on the street and not even notice."

"Did you notice anything else?"

"Not really."

"Glasses? Eye color? Build? Anything?"

"Nope. Sorry."

"Well, I am, too."

"You might try the courier company," the florist suggested, seeming to suffer a pang of conscience in the face of Alana's alarm.

"I will," she said, and hung up.

Alana felt angry with herself because she hadn't paid enough attention to the courier's uniform to remember which company he was with. After her first tentative calls to courier companies where she was asked for a worker ID number, she realized that she was getting nowhere. When she asked if they could trace the worker by identifying who had delivered any bouquets of dead flowers, she was crisply told such information was confidential and that the various firms had policies safeguarding their clienteles' privacy.

Alana was feeling increasingly bleak. Carrie noticed something was wrong when she came in to relieve Alana so that her friend would have time to change and eat before the community theater tryouts.

"Something's bothering you, Lannie," Carrie finally said, sighing. "I don't know what it is. But I'm here to listen to you if you want to talk."

Alana said nothing.

"Is it about Bill?" Carrie bravely ventured.

Alana gave a curt shake of her head.

"No, it's a personal problem that has nothing to do with Bill."

Or did it? The sudden thought ripped through her mind. As a master of disguise, even though Bill had natural looks that could turn any woman's head, he could present an innocuous, bland appearance that would render him all but invisible to the casual observer.

Carrie's scrutinizing gaze made Alana feel as if her friend was reaching right into her and unlocking her lips. She found herself speaking, even though she didn't want to, but she managed to contain the worst of her concerns.

"There's a situation that's alarming me. A personal problem, nothing to do with the business. I guess the bottom line is...I feel scared. Frightened. Vulnerable. It's not a pleasant feeling at all. I feel so helpless and unprotected."

"Ah," Carrie said. "Now I hear you." She moved to put an arm around Alana and gave her a comforting squeeze. "I used to feel like that before I realized that I could trust

Jesus to keep me safe, no matter what. As Christians, we can enjoy a wonderful sense of protection."

As miserable as she felt, Alana listened raptly to Carrie. She was so upset that she couldn't feel the natural hesitancy she usually sensed when her friend spoke about living a committed Christian life. Alana realized that she was too scared not to listen.

"I know that the Lord has a perfect plan for me," Carrie explained. "I know that I am His creation. I belong to Him. The Lord loves me, Alana, just as He does you. He wants the best for me. Sometimes, awful things happen, and I know that it is because the Lord has allowed them. God is sovereign, and He can make good things—miracles—arise out of tragic situations.

"When God allows evil to brush against us, it is only so that through the experience we may offer more perfect Christian witness, be drawn closer to Him, and enjoy a sense of knowing that we are protected even when we are in the most dangerous situations. We are *His*. The Lord cares for us as a loving father. This assurance is something committed Christians cherish. And it helps us to face scary situations without fear. Can you understand that?"

"Yes and no. It sounds good, but I'm not sure it works," Alana admitted.

"I know," Carrie commiserated. "I once felt that way, too. I know that there are others who can explain it better than I can. They could offer personal stories about how the

Lord has led them through some pretty rocky situations and eventually brought them happiness unlike anything they'd ever known."

"I could use a little of that."

"Tell you what," Carrie said, seeming emboldened. "My adult Sunday school class is made up of strong Christians, intellectually sharp folks, who love nothing better than a good discussion. I'd love it if you'd come to worship services and Sunday school with me this weekend, Alana. I know that if we raised the topic before such a diverse group, you'd surely get some insight to help you find serenity in any situation. How about it?"

"I don't know," Alana hedged.

"We could go out for a lovely lunch afterwards. And maybe find a museum exhibit or something neat to do to fill the afternoon. How about it? I can sweeten the deal even more," Carrie teased with a laugh, "if need be."

Alana managed a shaky smile. "Okay. It's a date. I'll do it," she agreed. "If I'm still here," she added so softly that her friend did not hear the bleak and fear-filled words.

seven

That evening, Alana felt a sense of trepidation as she left the warmth and light of the store to walk home alone. Carrie had insisted that Alana leave early and let Carrie close up the boutique. Part of Alana had wanted to stay at the store because she felt so much safer when she was with other people.

Reflecting on the day as she walked home, Alana was relieved that one of the first things she had done after receiving the hideous bouquet had been to rush outside and hurl it in the public trash can on the street corner. Because of that, Carrie hadn't discovered the bouquet. If she had, she would have peppered Alana with questions for which she had no answers concerning a situation about which she didn't dare speculate. Keeping the situation a secret seemed to Alana to be her best option.

Alana was cautious en route to her apartment, feeling glaringly aware of traffic approaching her. She stayed well onto the sidewalk to lessen the risk of a purposeful hit-and-run incident that could appear to bystanders as an accident.

"This is no way to live," she whispered morosely when she retrieved mail from her box in the lobby of the apartment building and caught herself worrying about a letter bomb. "You've got to stop thinking about it. Don't let yourself dwell on it, kid."

Her admonition was easier to give than to follow.

The red light on Alana's answering machine was not blinking when she arrived home, and she was relieved that there were no messages. Apparently her tormenter had not sought to terrify her at home as well as at work.

No sooner had Alana allowed herself a moment of relief than the telephone shrilled. Alana glanced at it and her throat tightened with alarm. She was tempted to let the machine take the call so that she could know who was on the line before she picked up the receiver. But she realized to do so would only allow the individual who was harassing her to exert further control over her life.

"Hello?" she answered, trying to sound as casual and serene as possible.

"Alana, it's Bill."

"Oh, Bill. Hi!" she said, suddenly feeling breathless with nervous tension.

"I called your store and Carrie told me that you had gone home early."

"Yes. Being one of the bosses has its privileges," she replied in a light tone.

"Last night Mark said that you were involved in the community theater. He told me about the tryouts being conducted tonight. I'm interested. I've already called the director—"

"I'm sure you'd be a welcome addition," Alana said, her voice sounding stiff even to her own ears. She felt a sudden pang. She thoroughly enjoyed her theater group, and she wasn't sure how she would handle it if Bill Sterling—the man she both loved and hated—was going to be a part of it.

"I'm looking forward to checking it out," he went on. "It's a good way to meet people and become part of the community. I like this area. I think I could happily live here for the rest of my life."

Bill Sterling? The man for whom the word "permanency" had seemed not to exist?

"I like it here," Alana said, to fill the silence that had stretched between them. Nervously she rose and paced her apartment, glancing down to the street below.

"When I talked to her, Carrie happened to mention that you'd walked home, that your car is due to go into the shop. So I figured I'd offer you transportation for the evening. How about it?"

"I don't know."

"Me—you know, Pet. A taxi driver you don't."

"What do you mean by that?" Alana asked, as her mind needled with suspicious thoughts.

"Only that you can count on me to get you to the theater and home again with no shilly-shallying."

"Oh. Well. I—"

"I'll tell you what. I'll pick you up at seven. Practice is at seven-thirty, isn't it?"

"Yes."

"Yes to both counts?"

Alana couldn't help smiling. "Yes to both questions."

"I'm on a roll," Bill said. "You know me: the inveterate risk-taker. How about going for broke and having dinner with me before we go to the theater?"

"Bill, I don't know," Alana stalled. She felt as if she were getting in over her head.

"Name the place and I'll take you there. Your desire can be fast food or haute cuisine, and I'm the man who'll willingly pick up the tab in order to enjoy your charming company again. With no strings attached."

"You mean that?"

"You can trust me, Alana, in a way that I realize you couldn't trust me before."

"Well, okay. Just don't read any more into this than is meant by my agreeing to have dinner with you," she warned, realizing that her voice sounded stern.

"Never, Alana. I'm grateful if I can hope for a second chance. I only want a shot at proving myself to be the man meant for you."

"You proved you weren't in the past. I don't know that you could ever prove that you are in the present."

"Just a chance. It's all I ask. Give me the chance, Alana, and Lord willing I'll erase all doubts from your mind."

For a response, Alana sighed, and the sound seemed to convince Bill to restrain himself before he pressed too hard.

"By the way, did you get the flowers?" At the mention of flowers, Alana felt her temper spike.

"You sent me flowers? Bill, how could you! Why did you do something like that?"

She thought of the horrible, dead flowers, and her heart ached anew. It seemed like an ugly joke that just when she'd considered the possibility of trusting Bill, he had admitted to being a cruel cad, beneath her contempt.

"Why? Because I love you," he whispered.

The emotions Alana had attempted to hold in all day suddenly spilled over with a deluge of hot tears and gulping sobs.

"My darling, why are you crying like that? Alana! Answer me," Bill demanded, his voice reflecting the frustration he felt because he wasn't with Alana and couldn't comfort her.

Just then, Alana saw a beige florist's van pull up to the curb in front of her apartment building. Her heart sank. Somehow, she just knew. Within three minutes, the buzzer sounded, signaling that she had a caller. Alana flipped open the security peephole and saw a delivery man staggering beneath a huge arrangement of roses.

"Someone's here, Bill. I'll be right back." Quickly Alana put down the receiver, undid the series of bolts, accepted the bouquet, and almost rudely shut the door in the deliveryman's face as she quickly redid the various locks. Picking up the receiver, she stammered, "That was th...the man from the florist's."

She pulled out the card from the tiny, waxed envelope. Bill's signature and tender sentiments stared up at her.

"The flowers just came. And they're lovely. Really lovely, Bill. Th...thank you."

"So do you like them?"

"I love them. Now...uh...I've really got to go. I'll see you tonight."

"Right. Dinner at six. See you then."

Even though Alana's heart was heavy with various concerns, she found herself excitedly looking through her wardrobe to find an outfit that would appeal to Bill but would also convince the director that she would be right for at least a supporting part in the musical production.

Finally Alana made her selection. She took extra care with her hair and makeup and was ready to go fifteen minutes before Bill was due to pick her up.

"You look lovely," he said upon his arrival.

"You look handsome yourself," she admitted, and found herself smiling up at him in a way she'd done long ago. Her heart tightened.

As if sensing her pain, Bill took her hand in his, pressed it in a quick clasp, and kept it in his warm grip as they went to his waiting car.

"Where do you want to go? What's milady's preference?"

"I have no idea. I don't even know what I want—"

Bill gave her a special look. "Well, in that case, it's up to me to persuade you to want what I want."

"You're incorrigible," Alana muttered.

Bill smiled. "Sure you don't have any preferences?"

Alana shook her head. "Not a one."

"Then I'd like to take you to this little restaurant that I just located. The food is great and the atmosphere is, too. When this place gets discovered by the general hordes, it'll probably ruin the ambience."

"You've been in town mere days and already you're discovering local treasures that have gone undetected by the natives?"

He shrugged. "It would seem so."

Alana couldn't help smiling. "Bill Sterling, some things never change."

"Some things about me haven't changed, my love, but the important aspects—the eternal considerations—have. I want to prove that to you. I want to convince you to let yourself love me again. I'll do whatever it takes so that you want to share my life, my faith, my love, and discover all that the Lord has created for us."

"That, my good fellow, is one very tall order," Alana pointed out in a tired tone.

"Lord willing," Bill said, and his voice took on a

warning edge, "I will do whatever it takes—whatever is required—to make that happen."

Alana gave him a quick glance. She wondered if it was fervor she heard in his voice or ruthlessness. The old Bill could be ruthless. In contrast, the new Bill seemed sincerely impassioned. But did he still possess the capability to be brutal? Did he want her back so badly that if he couldn't woo her return to his arms, he would attempt to frighten her back into his life?

eight

It was as if the years and the unpleasantness evaporated in the face of the warm conviviality that Alana and Bill shared over dinner. She almost hated for their moments alone to end. But soon it was time to get to the theater for the tryouts.

At the theater, Alana recognized a number of people she had performed with in the past. They rushed toward her and exchanged a flurry of hugs. Then Alana automatically introduced Bill, whom they cheerfully welcomed into their midst. The fact that Bill was apparently a friend of Alana's was a good enough recommendation for the group to accept him without reservation.

Alana noticed how well and easily Bill mixed with the group. She felt pride mixed with trepidation as she observed how some of the women sought even a crumb of his attention. Alana would have been alarmed, except that she was aware that Bill seemed to have eyes for only her.

"Okay. Everyone take seats," the director called out.

After some milling about, everyone finally found seats in the first few rows of the theater. The director took his place on stage, clipboard in hand. He paced back and forth as he explained their goals.

"I'm sure that we're all familiar with Rodgers and Hammerstein's wonderful musical, *Oklahoma!* It's a production that's always enthusiastically received, whether in a tiny rural hamlet or a large metropolitan area."

Quickly the director sketched in the basics. Then he outlined a production schedule, stage prop requirements, and set construction. He elaborated on the support people the production would need and explained that only a limited number of those present could expect to get acting parts in the performance, even though *Oklahoma!* was noted for a large cast.

"Not everyone can be a star every time," he pointed out.

Alana felt relief at that thought. She'd been the lead actress when they'd performed the somewhat high-brow *Romeo and Juliet,* and she'd had one of the leading roles in a few lesser-known works. With as many things as she had on her mind, she felt perfectly content—willing—to abandon her place center-stage and do her part working with the stage crew to make sure that the sets were as special as the performances that the actors and actresses were expected to deliver.

Alana scarcely listened as the director delivered instructions to those who wished to try out for the lead roles. She didn't get in any lines, but merely remained seated, as did Bill, who apparently didn't wish to arrive on his first night and seem to take over or give the impression that he expected to win the roles that seasoned actors in the close-knit community theater group assumed for their own.

"What?" The director stopped in front of Alana. "You're not going to try out tonight?"

"Well, yes, but...." In a quick rush of words, Alana explained that she'd had important parts in past productions and would be satisfied to work on the stage crew.

"Nonsense!" the director said. "While this is a nonprofit community organization, like everyone else, we have bills to pay. And you, Miss Charles, seem to be one of our star attractions. I know that your appearance in a production brings with it built-in sales. You have many loyal and adoring fans. Come, come, get in line."

Reluctantly Alana arose. The smile on her face was almost apologetic as she moved toward a line where those who wished to try out for the part of Laurey were queued up.

"And you, my good fellow," the director said, facing Bill. The man frowned. "Let me see." He studied Bill a long moment. "You could go either way. I could see you as a lighthearted and lovable Curly, or as a dark and sinister Jud Fry."

"Whatever you like," Bill pleasantly agreed, shrugging.

"Ever do any singing?" the director asked.

Bill shrugged. "A few solos in the church choir. Other than that, not much."

"Solos, eh?" the director repeated, and his attitude seemed to perk up. "Get in the line with those auditioning for Curly. And if I don't want to cast you in that part—there's always Judd."

The director spoke as if it were a foregone conclusion that Bill would get one part or the other.

When Alana auditioned for the part of Laurey, she didn't put her heart into it. She was too upset over the turn of events in her private life. But it seemed not to affect her performance.

"Break a leg, Alana!" Bill called out.

Alana tensed. Bill's good-luck greeting was the same as the message that had accompanied the horrid bouquet of dead flowers. She hadn't given the message any thought until that very moment, but it might prove to be a hint to the identity of the perverse individual who was tormenting her.

Could Bill have sent the dead bouquet and then ordered the lovely arrangement of roses to allay her suspicions? Was he so intent on winning her back? Did he hope that she would be alarmed by the dead bouquet, comforted by the lovely arrangement of fresh flowers, and believe him to be a man in whom she could trust—one she could turn to for comfort and protection?

Alana forced the questions from her mind as she mounted the steps to the stage and focused on the audition she was about to give.

"Good luck, my darling!" sang out one of the community theater's fans, an elderly woman, swathed in mink and diamonds, who had a younger, apparently shy man at her side. Alana had overheard the man offer to work on the flats for the set, locate necessary props, or serve as a prompter.

Not wanting Bill to detect that she had misgivings about trusting him, Alana forced herself to flash Bill a grin, one that flicked to include the dowager philanthropist and the shy new addition to the community theater group who was standing next to her. The young man seemed awed that he was surrounded by theater people, so close to the action.

Alana also noticed the individuals—theater backers— who had come forward, purse strings loosened, to rescue the theater group's productions in the past when the group had run short of funds. Those financial supporters expressed enthusiasm when Alana completed her audition.

"Bravo!"

"Encore!"

"There's your star!"

Alana felt her face flush, but she was nonetheless pleased.

She took a seat, and moments later, Bill sat down beside her. He had been wonderful as he'd played the part of Curly. Alana realized that she had blocked from her mind how wonderfully talented, natural actor he was.

When it was Bill's turn to audition as the sinister Jud Fry,

Alana felt a tingle of alarm and apprehension sweep over her at the transformation that took place before her eyes. Bill mussed his hair, lowered his face, and seemed to collect his thoughts for a moment. Then when he faced the audience, it was as if he had really become the rough, ruthless Jud Fry. Bill's eyes glowed with a savage glint, and Alana found herself feeling almost afraid of him. Bothersome possibilities crept into her mind.

Bill had told her that he was a changed man. But could he so quickly and easily bring forth an evil persona if he were as different as he claimed?

Alana felt a headache building at her temples as she took a quiet seat toward the back of the auditorium. The young man who had accompanied the elderly woman approached her.

"You seem to be feeling unwell," he observed. "Can I get you something?"

"I...I'll be fine," Alana said, and gave him a weak smile.

"You're sure?" His eyes were kind and solicitous.

She nodded. "Positive."

"Well, if you're sure. We don't want our favorite leading lady to suffer, now, do we?" He gave Alana a friendly pat on the shoulder as he passed by. "You're a shoo-in for Laurey, Miss Alana. It's only a matter of time before the director announces that. The other girls don't stand a chance. There's no one but you...no one but you. I've been one of your major fans, Miss Charles, and I look forward to being a part of the community theater and getting to know everyone involved."

"How kind of you to say such nice things. I'm sure we'll appreciate your talents as you're able to assist us," Alana replied, smiling pleasantly as he wandered off and Bill came to collect her. They moved down to the front rows again, the better to hear the director as he assigned the roles.

"Alana Charles and Bill Sterling, please come forward!"

Bill arose, then gallantly turned back to offer Alana his arm.

"Ladies and gentlemen," the director said in such a dramatic tone that they could almost hear a drum roll. "The stars for *Oklahoma!*: Alana Charles as Laurey, and the area's newest male thespian talent—Bill Sterling—as Curly."

A round of applause went up, almost drowning out the director as he cried out the role call of other actresses and actors who had been assigned parts ranging from Aunt Eller to Ado Annie to Will to Jud.

"Pick up copies of the script," the director finished up his instructions ten minutes later. "Our first practice will be at the regularly scheduled time. This is a challenging production, so be sure to prepare on your own time. See you all a week from tonight—with bells on."

"Ready to go, Miss Laurey?" Bill asked, grinning down

at Alana.

"Your hair's a bit straight, but somehow, I think I like you better as Curly than as the sinister Jud Fry."

"I'm more content being gentle than sinister, myself," Bill murmured, and Alana sensed that he referred to more than the play in which they were stars.

"It looks like I've got my work cut out for me. Until tonight, I've done little more than sing in the shower and warble along with hit tunes on the radio," Alana admitted.

"You're a natural, my dear," Bill assured.

"At least you've had some practice," Alana retorted, "singing in front of church congregations." She shook her head. "Somehow I have a hard time reconciling that picture with the Bill Sterling I used to know."

"You could get a little experience that way, too, Pet. Mark invited me to go to their church's choir practice. I may see if there's room for another baritone. I'm sure that they could always use a gorgeous soprano."

"Thanks for the suggestion," Alana said, hoping that the chill she felt didn't enter her voice. "But I'm not ready to commit myself to anything else at this time."

"Commitment." Bill spoke the word reflectively. "You know, that's really the name of the game. Commitment to Christ. I'd like to tell you about my experience."

Alana didn't want to hear Bill's story, but the way his eyes were shining, she sensed that it meant a great deal to him. She simply didn't have the heart to let him know that while at one time she also had found the idea exciting, now it only held memories of loss and abandonment.

"Maybe some other time," she deflected his desire.

In response Bill gave her another grin. "I can bide my time. The Lord was patient in His wait for me; I can be patient as I wait for you."

Alana was about to make a retort, but Bill already had changed the topic.

"You just made me a very happy man," he said.

Alana glanced at him.

"I did? How?"

"When you replied 'some other time.' " His smile deepened. "That gives me hope that you are going to give me a second chance, that you will agree to spend more time with me. Will you?"

"I don't know, Bill," Alana admitted. "Maybe yes. Maybe no. At this moment, I'm just not sure."

"But I can call you, okay?"

"Okay. And...and Bill, I'm thinking about using my machine to screen all calls," Alana admitted, suddenly not wanting to risk missing him because he would hang up the phone rather than leave a message.

He gave her an assessing, PI stare. "Been having some trouble that I should know about, Pet?"

She looked away from him. She had to. If she met his eyes, either she'd burst into tears and sob out the entire story or he'd know that the woman he professed to love was a liar.

"No," she said, glancing away from him. "It's just rather nice to know who's on the line before you pick up the receiver. It cuts down on a lot of nuisance calls at mealtime when telemarketers seem to do their most hard-sell solicitations."

"Oh. Okay," Bill said, apparently accepting her explanation. "I'll be sure to identify myself—and leave a message if you're not home."

They fell into silence as they crossed the dim parking lot toward Bill's waiting car. Alana felt the tension that thrummed between them.

They were to the rear of Bill's car when suddenly he halted. In the darkness his hand felt for hers. He pulled her to him, and as cold, velvety mist swirled around their faces, his warm lips came down on hers. Then his arms slid around her, making her feel so cherished, so loved, so protected, that Alana never wanted to leave his embrace again.

Bill seemed lost in their kiss.

But when Alana heard squealing tires, thoughts of them being run down by a crazy, psychotic hit-and-run driver overtook her, and she almost trampled Bill in her hysterical alarm to break away from him and dart for safety.

"Alana, lighten up," Bill chided.

"I...I thought—" She clamped her lips shut before she was reduced to paranoid, babbling gibberish that could reveal her sordid fears and the strange situation that left her constantly feeling in jeopardy.

"It's only kids hot rodding on the city streets. No biggie. But I'm glad to know you have such excellent reactions," he teased. "Maybe you can take care of yourself after all, milady."

"Maybe," Alana agreed, forcing a smile. At the moment she couldn't remember a time when she had felt so vulnerable or terrified. If, after another week went by, she was still jumping out of her skin over the least little thing, she was going to call her physician and ask for a mild sedative. She knew she needed something. But she didn't know what.

And part of her still rebelled against the philosophy that Carrie, Mark—and now Bill—professed. That regardless of what the problem, Jesus Christ was the solution.

nine

Although Alana had expected to sleep poorly after Bill took her home, to her surprised relief, after a warm shower and a light bedtime snack, she slipped between the sheets and was asleep almost before her head hit the pillow.

She had felt a giddy sense of relief when she had checked her machine and found no messages had been phoned in during her absence. As an added bonus, her night's sleep was unbroken by any random crank calls.

Perhaps, she thought with a sense of optimism when she arose the next morning, her tormentor had chosen to focus his attentions on someone else. Or maybe he had decided to desist altogether. She could hope so.

As she worked through her day at the shop without encountering any alarming incidents, Alana felt a sense of confidence sweep over her. When the next day was as serene, her good feelings increased. By the time she faced the weekend, Alana had convinced herself that the entire episode was an alarming incident that belonged to the past.

Ordinarily, Alana used weekends to get caught up on tasks around her apartment, but she had a full day ahead of her on Sunday. She had agreed to accompany Mark and

Carrie to church services and to their adult Sunday school class.

It had been many years since Alana had attended worship services except for obligatory appearances at Christmas and Easter. She was surprised by how many people she knew—and by how warmly they greeted her. It felt wonderful to be invited back so enthusiastically.

When she had seen Bill seated across the aisle, down toward the front, Alana had felt momentary unease, but she forced herself to concentrate on the pastor's sermon and immerse herself in the choir's inspiring renditions instead of dwelling on her puzzling relationship with an old love.

In the classroom where the adults gathered for Sunday school, Alana took a chair. As the discussion began, she soon realized that she was not as knowledgeable about the Bible as she liked to think of herself, and she was forced to admit that most of the other adults in the room had studied the Bible until they knew it well and were able to discuss it with insight and intelligence. Alana's eyes flicked to Carrie's when her friend cleared her throat.

"This week," Carrie said, "I had a friend who was very frightened by a situation and was feeling alone, vulnerable, and unsafe. I tried to explain about the Lord's protection of His people, but I fear I didn't do a tremendously good job.

"I got to thinking that perhaps I don't understand the

concept as well as I should, or I'd have felt more competent
in getting it across to my friend. I know that I have a very
good feeling—a security—in realizing that the Lord is
taking care of me, no matter what. I thought if any of you
have ideas to share, relevant Scripture, or personal testimonies, it might be helpful if we could have sort of a
round-table discussion."

"Great idea!" someone said.

"I'd like to address that topic," a young woman inter-
jected.

Alana said nothing, but she listened with all her heart.
She felt tears burn behind her eyes as she listened to their
various stories. They were average people, a lot like she
considered herself. To have looked at outward appearances, she would never have dreamed that they had faced
traumas in their lives that were as terrifying, in various
ways, as what she had known.

They had felt abandoned. They, too, had been made
exhausted by fear and tension. But they had turned to the
Lord and found their strength and security in their relationship with Him.

Alana stared at the floor as Bill began to tell his story,
one where he admitted that he'd been a soldier of fortune,
a hired killer who traveled to foreign countries to work to
overthrow dictatorial, brutal regimes.

"The Lord saw within me a different man than I saw
myself," Bill said, "for I followed my own vices and

worldly desires. I had a reputation of being courageous beyond question. But believe me, I had moments of being weak with fear when I stared death—my own death—in the face. I knew what it was to be frightened. I thought I was a strong man, and I was. I could bench press with the best of them, run in marathons, use martial arts, but looking back I'm appalled at how weak I was.

"I realize now that the Lord knew one day I would be His, even though I had never once given any thought to my need for God. I certainly hadn't considered committing myself to Christ, accepting Him as my Savior, and living my life as He would want me."

Although Alana couldn't—wouldn't—meet Bill's eyes, her ears strained to hear every word of his dramatic and dangerous tale involving foreign intrigue, hired assassins, and a kill-or-be-killed scenario.

"I knew that my hours were numbered. I knew that I was going to die," Bill said. "First my captors, I was sure, were going to torture me until I told them everything I knew. I was working as an emissary of free world interests. There were a lot of the enemy—and only one of me. I had a capsule that I had been given and ordered to swallow if my capture looked inevitable. But I'd lost it in the scuffle. So I didn't have a way out." Bill paused and his voice grew husky with emotion.

"As I realized that death was hours away, that the rest of my life could be numbered in minutes, I started to think back over what I had accomplished in life.

"What? Nothing. At least nothing that mattered. And I'd done many things for which I was suddenly deeply ashamed. Among them, walking out on the woman I loved, leaving her at the altar of a church while I flew off to take that last assignment—the high-paying, high-risk job that would provide me enough money so that I could pursue the career I wanted and live in luxury.

"I knew I was going to die, and I felt tears overwhelm me as I realized I hadn't even known how to really live. I started to think of the things I'd learned in Sunday school almost twenty-five years earlier, when I'd attended classes like those your children are in today," he said, gesturing in the direction of the children's department.

"Scripture came back to me, and I realized suddenly, overwhelmingly, that I was not alone. The Lord God promised never to leave us, never to forsake us, to be there, our shield and our comfort, if only we would hide ourselves in Him.

"I knew I didn't have much time left, but at that moment, I turned my life over to the Lord. I trustingly placed my life, all that I was, all that I would ever be, in His care. As I did, I knew a serenity unlike anything I had ever experienced.

"I realized that I only had a few hours left, but I wanted those hours to belong to the Lord. I wanted to live as He would have me do, not exist by the wits and wiles of my worldly, mercenary career.

"I prayed to God to heal the people I'd injured in life, those I'd disappointed, those I'd harmed, intentionally and by accident. It was the most wonderful, uplifting experience of my life when I gave myself to the Lord, committed myself to Him, and accepted Him into my heart.

"I knew I was a sinner. I knew how unworthy I was. I didn't even dare hope that I would be spared what I realized I faced. But after much Bible study, I now know, as do you all, that the Lord has a special purpose for each and every one of us.

"Although I was prepared to die, it wasn't my time. The Lord God intended me to live on and serve Him as I had previously served only the people who could pay me.

"The Lord protected me. Many people, I know, do not believe that miracles happen in this day and age, but we know better. That day, in a hot, bug-infested, snake-populated jungle, the Lord worked many miracles for me. Too many for me to go into in our limited time here.

"But the Lord protected me, kept me safe, and brought me out of that hostile and foreign land, just as He protected His children in the Old Testament, safely bringing them out of unfriendly nations to the land of milk and honey.

"Those of you fortunate enough to be parents are aware of how you nurture your little children, keep them safe, and protect them to the best of your ability. As good a job as we adults do in trying to protect our children, our minds cannot begin to grasp how our Heavenly Father is prepared to protect His beloved children."

"Thanks for sharing, Bill," Carrie said and reached across to squeeze his hand.

Alana was touched. She tried to steel herself against the onslaught of emotions she felt as she imagined Bill in the straits that he had described, knowing that he'd put himself in such peril because long ago he'd wanted to provide worldly goods, material possessions, and afford financial security for her and for himself. She hardly heard the other stories that people told, everyday instances so different from Bill's cloak-and-dagger tale.

Too soon, it seemed, their Sunday school teacher offered a closing prayer and the morning's activities at church drew to a close. Bill was surrounded by a knot of people who wanted to offer input about his experiences or hear more. Alana, Carrie, and Mark were preparing to leave when Mark sidetracked to approach Bill.

"Got any plans for the day?" Mark asked.

"As a matter of fact, no," Bill said.

"Would you care to join us for dinner?" Mark asked. "It's just Carrie, Alana, and me. We'd all love to have your company."

Bill looked at Carrie who gave him a bright nod. From Mark's warm hand on his shoulder, he knew his friend's sentiment. His eyes flicked to Alana's, and she saw a residue of pain and knew that Bill would not inflict his company on her if she truly did not desire it.

After hearing the pastor's sermon centering on forgiveness, she was mellowed. She gave a faint smile and an almost imperceptible nod, signaling to Bill that his company was welcome.

Bill's smile of relief and joy nicely rivaled the noonday sun that had peeped through the cloud cover, spreading light over what had, the week before, seemed to be an ominous, foreboding, and threat-filled world.

ten

As Alana looked back over the month of January, she was amazed by all that had happened since Bill Sterling had reentered her life mere days after the new year had begun. Her life was busy—brimming with activities as never before—and she found herself content and invigorated in a new way.

Business was booming at the Shoestring Boutique. Alana knew that she needed to take a buying trip to replenish the unique and trendy items that the store offered in addition to classic apparel. But that trip would have to be postponed until after the final curtain call for *Oklahoma!* unless she made arrangements for an understudy to take her part during the ten days required for her to visit the major markets. It would take at least that long to look over the new offerings, make her selections, and fill out purchase orders.

Alana's personal life was as full as her professional existence. She found herself having more commitments than ever. After attending the church potluck held before the concert, she had received invitations to every dinner the church planned. Getting into the spirit of things, Alana had dug out one of her late mother's best recipes and prepared a casserole that earned rave reviews.

"She cooks like this and she's still single?" Mark teased, winking at Bill.

"Ah, but you should see what culinary damage I can do on a bad day," Alana retorted, sending Mark a warning look which she hoped was playful enough so that he wouldn't become offended, but clear enough so that he would understand that she didn't want him trying to marry her off.

Carrie had been after Alana to join a Bible study, but she begged off.

"There are only twenty-four hours in a day, the last I knew," Alana said. "I'm committed to the max. I'm putting in full-time hours at the boutique, and I have play practice twice a week. That's not to mention hours of my own time devoted to studying lines and going over the music scores."

"I can't wait until opening night," Carrie said.

"It's going to be wonderful," Alana predicted. "I've starred in so many of the community theater's productions that I've been feeling a bit guilty. The stage hands and set-builders work so hard but get too little credit. So a couple of evenings a night, I'm going to the auditorium and helping them nail together flats, paint the rural scenery, and attend to some of the less glamorous jobs."

"That's thoughtful of you."

"Not really. I'm glad to do it. I'm getting to know the supporting staff much better. I'm making a few close friends."

"Anyone we should know about?" Carrie asked, winking. "We don't want you springing any surprises on us."

"Just a girlfriend or two," Alana admitted, then named some names. Carrie knew one, had heard of the other, but had no recollection of ever having heard of the third.

"We go out for coffee afterwards or order a pizza. It's pleasant. And I felt that I really needed to broaden my horizons and develop a social life that didn't include business associates from the boutique or people from your church."

"It's not my church," Carrie said. "At least not in the way you seemed to mean it. You have as much a right to be there as anyone. The Lord wants your presence there as much as, maybe even more than, He does the regulars who've built, maintained, and nurtured the congregation and building."

"I suppose so," Alana said, but she felt vaguely uncomfortable with the way the conversation was going. Carrie seemed to sense her mood.

"So you're meeting some nice women at the theater? Met any likely guys?"

"No, but then I haven't been looking."

"Ah, Bill's had something to say about that?"

Alana tensed.

"Bill has nothing to say about that," she said, her tone stiff. "He doesn't control my time. He has no options on me. We've spent a good deal of time together, yes, but it's professional in nature. At least that is how I feel about it. Bill's view is his own and is of no interest to me."

"You don't have to be touchy," Carrie said. "I was only being conversational."

"And I suppose I was only being a bit defensive," Alana admitted. "The past being what it was...I know there are people who are aware of the situation and who are only too willing to make assumptions." She paused. "And, unfortunately, Bill Sterling may be one of them."

"He does treat you rather possessively, doesn't he?" Carrie acknowledged. "I would imagine that with Bill at your side, sticking to you like a cockleburr, it would certainly dissuade the approach of some other fellow whose eye you caught."

"There's no one at the theater that interests me in that way," Alana said, "although there is one guy I've gotten to know. He's pleasant enough and I think he'd like to ask me out, but he's not my type."

"Really? Do tell," Carrie encouraged.

"Not much to tell. I'm pleasant to him. But I don't really encourage him. And if he seems to be working toward building up the courage to ask me out, then I deftly change the subject. I'd rather avoid giving him the opportunity to ask me out than have to find a tactful way to turn him down.

It seems easier that way."

Carrie smiled. "How well I remember that art. I've done it myself a few times over the years."

"So, have you seen Bill?" Alana asked.

"No. Not since services Sunday morning." She frowned. "You mean you haven't?"

"Uh-uh. We'd been planning to practice together at the boutique one night. We figured we could sing at the store after hours and not disturb anyone, as we'd risk doing at either my apartment or his. The acoustics aren't the best, but the after-hours privacy is what we need. And we didn't want to go to the auditorium and get in the way of the stage crews."

"So? Did he stand you up? That doesn't sound like Bill."

"No, nothing like that. But he did leave a message on my machine that something came up. That can mean anything." Alana gave a bitter laugh. "In the past I received any number of those messages. He would promise to get in touch later, and 'later' might mean within the hour, or days, or even a few weeks. The last time, of course, stretched out to be two years."

"But Bill's different now," Carrie defended. "And he is working to establish a new business. PI's don't work nine to five, and they must be discreet. If he's doing an investigation, he has to be careful, not even confiding in those he trusts."

"I'm not sure that he trusts me any more than I trust

him," Alana said.

"Drop a remark like that in my presence," Carrie said, "and I definitely pick it up. Okay, come clean, my friend: what are you driving at?"

"Bill's watching me."

"Of course he is," Carrie said. "It doesn't take a rocket scientist to figure out that one. Anyone in the same room with you two soon discovers that the fellow can't take his eyes off you."

"That's not what I meant," Alana said. "Bill's watching me."

"Watching you? As in stakeouts? Surveillance? That type of thing?"

Alana nodded. "I think so."

"What makes you believe that?"

"Things. Odd things. Carrie, there have been strange occurrences in my life since right before Bill walked into the boutique that day and reentered my life like a one-man SWAT team. I realize now that it was Bill behind those incidents. I didn't know it at the time. There were...suspicious...things going on. Situations that I haven't confided in you.

"I've given it long and careful thought, and I think Bill's the one behind the acts. He pretends to be my friend while scaring me like an enemy. He acts like he's a staunch supporter, but behind the scenes I have good reason to suspect he's a detractor. It's a clever attempt to manipulate me so that he gets what he wants—or thinks he wants—out of life."

"Have you told Bill your suspicions?"

"Of course not—and don't you, either." Alana's voice took on scorn. "I wouldn't dream of spoiling his James Bond, 007, Magnum PI fun and games!"

"Lannie, you know I care about you and that I find you an extremely credible person, or I wouldn't be in business with you. But I have a very hard time believing that Bill Sterling could be pulling any stunts on you. I've found him to be open and honest. I know that Mark has, too. We trust him implicitly."

"Of course," Alana said in a cool tone. "That act makes it all the easier to snooker trusting, unsuspecting people. Well, Bill's fooled me in the past, but he won't get a chance to trick me again. I'll never trust that man, no matter how long I live—and no matter how many people tell me what a fine Christian he is."

"It bothers you that he's become a committed Christian, doesn't it?" Carrie asked.

"Of course not!" Alana protested, but a hot, prickly flush seeped over her features, making her feel uncomfortable. Carrie had cut to the core of the matter more quickly, and far more directly, than Alana liked.

The truth was, she didn't like Bill's Christian commitment. It felt like a double betrayal. The first time Bill had thrown her over for a country. Then before he came back, he'd thrown her over for God—a powerful Being whose love Alana couldn't bring herself to trust.

"The fact that Bill is a committed Christian doesn't steal something away from your basic relationship, Alana." Carrie's words interrupted Alana's thoughts. "In fact, when a man and woman share not only a love for each other but also an abiding faith and love for the Lord, it enriches the human love they know. It makes it into something that is treasured and enduring."

"Little matter, for I don't love Bill Sterling. I did in the past, but I'll never be that stupid again."

"Why do you think he's keeping you under surveillance?" Carrie asked.

Alana gave a short-tempered wave of her hand.

"With Bill, who knows? Maybe he figures I'm Metro-St. Louis's answer to Mata Hari."

"Is he jealous?"

"I wouldn't think so," Alana said. "Between my hours at the boutique and at play practice, I haven't had much time to foster any other social relationships except impromptu lunch or coffee dates with people from the theater."

"Then I think you're probably mistaken," Carrie said.

"I know what I saw," Alana maintained, her voice terse.

"What did you see?"

"A car, *Bill's car*, parked in a surreptitious manner where my apartment building—and my comings and goings—could be monitored with ease."

"Believe what you want," Carrie said. "I know that I can't change your mind. But I've come to trust my instincts, and I have faith in Bill Sterling."

"I've also come to trust my instincts," Alana said. "I've gotten into 'conditioning' and 'learned behavior.' A stormy past with Bill Sterling taught me—and taught me well—not to trust him as far as I could throw him."

"I think you should confront Bill, Alana. If he is watching you, I'm sure that he has a very good reason. And if someone else is spying on you, we really need to know who it is."

"I'm not saying a word to Bill," Alana said, "and if you wish to stay my friend and business partner, you won't say anything to him either. And I mean it!" she affirmed, her eyes flashing.

"Bill Sterling walked into my life begging me to give him a second chance. Well, I'm not only giving him a second chance, I'm also giving him enough rope to hang himself! Some things never change, and I imagine that the basic Bill Sterling is one of them."

"I think you're making a mistake," Carrie quietly added, although it was clear she wasn't going to jeopardize her business relationship or personal friendship by crossing any boundaries.

Alana gave a bitter laugh.

"I've made plenty of mistakes in the past. That's why

I'm so cautious now, my friend. Remember what they say? 'Fool me once—shame on you. Fool me twice—shame on me!' Believe me, it won't happen again. Now, excuse me while I phone the director and ask him to get a second understudy for my part, because I really do need to fly to New York on a buying trip." Alana paused and quirked a brow. "Unless you'd like to do the honors this season."

"Count me out," Carrie said. "It's your sense of style and pizazz and eye for what's hot in the marketplace that's keeping us solvent."

"We really are a good pair," Alana said. "And I'm sorry if I get testy sometimes. But it feels good to let you know exactly how I feel."

"Hey—it's good for relationships, pal. Factor most broken relationships down to their lowest common denominator, and lack of honesty is the major reason for failure." Carrie paused. "I think Bill Sterling is ready to get honest with you. But it appears you're not ready, or even willing, to get honest with him."

"At the moment, you're right. I'm not even willing to consider becoming willing."

eleven

The next night was play rehearsal. Alana still had not heard from Bill, and eventually she concluded that there was no reason that she should. After all, he had no obligations to her. He was merely an old friend from the past and owed her no more fealty in the future than she owed him.

And, come to think of it, she had told him repeatedly that she wasn't interested in being won back or in picking up where they had left off, so perhaps he had finally taken her at her word and was shifting his focus elsewhere. There were any number of women at church, committed Christians like he was, who would have welcomed a call from Bill.

To Alana's relief, she hadn't felt such a strong sensation of being watched during the preceding few days, and when she'd carefully scanned the streets in as innocent and unassuming a manner as possible, she hadn't spotted Bill's car surreptitiously parked so that it was all but unnoticed by the casual observer.

Alana swung her car into the auditorium parking lot for play practice. Her heart skipped a beat when she noticed that Bill's vehicle was already in the lot. She walked into the auditorium, approached the cluster of people gathered for play practice, but didn't see Bill right away. She decided that perhaps he was in the restroom or conferring with the director back stage.

Alana was involved in a conversation with Missy Starwalt and other crew members when the director summoned Missy to his office area. Gordon Walters, the shy fellow who had accompanied his philanthropist mother to the auditions, remained with Alana as others drifted away to undertake their assigned duties.

"Everything is shaping up beautifully, Miss Charles. The director should be pleased. Mother's been happy with my reports."

Alana touched his arm, laughing lightly.

"Please, I've told you before to call me Alana. 'Miss Charles' sounds so formal and unfriendly. You make me feel old," she said, giving a wry chuckle. "And I know we're probably around the same age."

Gordon Walters blushed deep red.

"Very well, Alana it is. But only if you'll call me Gordy."

"I'll be glad to, Gordy," she replied. "And I must agree, the various flats are looking wonderful. You've been a welcome addition to our theater group."

"I'm glad you like them. We're doing our utmost. We feel that it's only appropriate to do the best possible job to create an appropriate setting to cameo our favorite leading lady: you."

At that instant, Missy came bursting out from the director's office, pirouetted, shrieked with glee, and hugged herself as she leaped into the air and came down with gleaming eyes.

"Guess what? I'm going to be a star!" Missy cried with excitement. "I'm replacing Lannie for the opening night performance! I'm so excited I can hardly stand it." Her radiant-eyed gaze swung around to include them all. "I promise you, I'm going to be great! The best!"

There was a quick flutter of conversation among the cast members. Bill, who had just entered the theater from the outside, arrived in time to hear Missy's unexpected announcement. He shot Alana a questioning look which she deflected by obliquely staring through him. She quickly turned to Gordy as if what he said was the most fascinating, riveting comment on earth.

Alana didn't consider it necessary for the entire cast to know that she had asked the director to give her a second understudy to guarantee that there would be someone else to play Laurey on opening night.

She had told the director that business interests forced the decision. She had also asked him to keep their conversation confidential, stressing that there was no reason for the rank-and-file cast members to know every aspect of the business behind a production when she considered her decision to be no one else's business.

From the director's lack of response when cast members barraged him with questions, Alana knew her secret was safe with him. Her secret, that is, to the extent that she had chosen to reveal it. Granted, she needed to go on a buying trip for the boutique, but she could have safely postponed the venture until after *Oklahoma!* had enjoyed its planned run in the area.

What she couldn't postpone, she decided, was the necessity to distance herself from Bill Sterling. He had warned her that, Lord willing, he would make her fall in love with him again. What he didn't realize, and Alana now knew only too well, was that it was impossible. Bill could hardly make her fall in love with him again when she had never stopped loving him.

Alana wanted to guard her heart, to keep her distance. But until the past week, she had been seeing entirely too much of Bill Sterling to make herself comfortable. She saw him at church and at dinner with Carrie and Mark afterwards; she was with him at play practice and at their private rehearsals.

Even her personal time wasn't safe. Alana never knew when Bill was going to bop into the boutique or stop by her apartment with some contrived bit of musical-related business, like when he showed up at her apartment with a video of *Oklahoma!* for them to watch and when he'd dropped by the store to give her a CD of the score to the musical so she could sing along with it and learn the words in the privacy of her apartment.

A week apart, she had hoped, would increase her resistance. But when she saw Bill at rehearsal, she suffered that old weak-at-the-knees, pounding-heart syndrome. Clearly she wasn't immune to his presence.

Alana both dreaded and anticipated Bill's approach, and she knew that it was only a matter of time. She was aware that he would ask her out for coffee after practice. Or would he? Perhaps he hadn't seen her during the past week because he was involved with someone else.

"What's the idea of that?" Gordy hissed, his normally placid, benign personality aroused. "Look at her! Making such a public spectacle of herself," he clucked over Missy's behavior. "Has she no sense of decorum? No idea of how blatantly egotistically she's behaving? Has she no consideration for your feelings?"

"Shhhh," Alana again touched his arm, shushing him. "Let her enjoy the limelight."

Gordy gave her an unbelieving look.

"Limelight, I might point out, that she's enjoying because she's stolen from you! It's anyone's guess what she did to get the director to take away your moment of triumph and give it to her." Then he adopted an indifferent, accepting air.

"Well, someday she'll get hers," he said. "Just don't you worry. That type always does—although sometimes a long time passes before the likes of her get their comeuppance!" Gordy harumphed in disgusted contempt.

Alana didn't hear exactly what he said next, but she nodded vague agreement as she focused her attention elsewhere. She didn't—couldn't—answer, for at that moment Bill proceeded directly toward her.

"Long time, no see, Alana." Bill repeated the line he had said the day he first walked into the Shoestring Boutique. "Can we get together for coffee after the rehearsal?"

"Well, I—" she began.

"No you can't!" Gordon said with quiet authority, answering for her. He took a protective step toward Alana. "She just agreed to go out to coffee with me."

"That's right, Bill. Sorry, but Gordon just now asked me out."

She saw the stab of regret in Bill's eyes and a different light that glowed. Hurt? Jealousy? Little matter, for Alana realized that now Bill knew how it felt. A perverse part of her enjoyed his discomfort.

Suddenly, she saw a way that she could rid herself of Bill Sterling and his influence over her life. She could spend more time with Gordy. He didn't make her pulse quicken, he didn't make her knees feel weak. But he was nice, he was considerate, and he was well-educated. His attitudes were sincere, whereas Alana had learned long ago not to trust Bill Sterling.

"Care to make it a threesome?" Bill asked, and Alana realized how desperate he seemed in protecting what he possessively considered his interests.

Gordy didn't look happy with the prospect, but was too much the gentleman to refuse if Alana wished that Bill join them. Recognizing how eagerly Gordy had been looking forward to time alone with her so that they could become better acquainted, she cast the shy heir a smile and gave Bill a carefully apologetic look.

"As a matter of fact, I'd like to have some time alone with Gordy, Bill. Sorry," she said, but the lilting look in her eyes didn't look at all apologetic.

"Some other time," Bill said in an off-hand manner as if it made no difference to him, but deep down in his eyes, Alana saw proof that it did.

Missy Starwalt, who had overheard the exchange, boldly inserted herself into the conversation.

"I'd love to go out for coffee with you, Mr. Sterling," she murmured. "If you don't mind? It could be ever so helpful to me, I know, since we'll be starring opposite one another."

Bill appeared to consider the potential benefits of a coffee date. "Very well, Missy. Coffee afterwards."

"Ohhh! I'm so excited!" Missy trilled. "Starring on opening night, and now a date with the leading man!"

That night, both Alana and Bill's performances were off. Alana realized that, Christian though he might be, Bill was steaming angry, and that fact did her heart good. Finally she had gotten beneath his skin, and she enjoyed watching the payback for all the hurt and humiliation he'd heaped on her in the past.

When the night's rehearsal concluded and it was time to leave, Alana could not have asked for a more gallant escort than Gordy Walters. He walked her to her car, tucked her in, and named the place where they would meet for an intimate cup of coffee. Then he disappeared down the line of cars toward his own vehicle.

To Alana's relief, their destination was not the restaurant she and Bill had frequented. But part of her desired to flaunt the fact that she was out with another man while Bill was having coffee with Missy Starwalt.

"A table for two," Gordon told the hostess. He touched Alana's elbow as they were guided to the table and helped her with her chair.

"Two coffees, black," Gordy told the waitress after conferring with Alana. "Anything else, dear girl? Pie? Cake? A sandwich? Bowl of soup?"

"Nothing, thanks," Alana said.

"I'll have a piece of that black walnut Italian cream cake I saw in the display case," Gordy said.

"Coming right up," the waitress said as she wrote the information on an order ticket.

Gordy reached across the table and laid his hand over Alana's.

"I'm so distressed over the director's naming Missy Starwalt to replace you for the opening run of the play. I can only imagine how you feel, dear girl. I've a notion to report the incident to Mother. She's one of the group's major benefactors, and the director owes his position—a very well-paid position—to her. She won't be pleased with your being bumped from the starring role so a brassy girl like Missy Starwalt can benefit. I'm upset! Mother will be, too."

Alana felt a twinge of alarm that Gordy was making a mountain out of a mole hill. She was tempted to offer explanations but realized that she didn't want to. Gordy was upset at the moment, but with the dawning of a new day, he would probably have the situation in the right perspective. Missy's euphorically egotistical behavior had probably irritated him more than someone accustomed to dealing with people from all walks of life.

"Don't be upset, Gordy," Alana said softly. "It's not important. Truly, it's not."

"But it *is*," Gordy insisted. "I don't like what was done to you, my darling. I don't like it at all!"

"Don't concern yourself with it, Gordy," Alana said. "It's not your problem." She was again tempted to tell him the truth, but she censored herself before she could. She knew that Carrie recommended honesty in all dealings and believed it to be essential for building strong, enduring relationships, but while Alana wanted Gordy as a casual friend—no one wanted to collect enemies—she did not want to trust him with her most private feelings and decisions.

"That may be impossible, Alana, for you're the kind of girl—so sweet, so gentle, so good—that when you have a problem, I want it to become *my* problem. I want to handle it for you and keep you safe. I've never known a girl like you before. I'm a great admirer of yours, both personally and professionally. Being with you like this is a culmination of my fondest fantasy."

Alana felt a twinge of guilt. Gordy seemed so pleasant, and although he had obviously been born with a silver spoon in his mouth and his mother could lay the world at his feet, he was a simple, down-to-earth person. It took so little to make him happy.

"That's sweet of you to feel that way," Alana said. "Many people wouldn't. It's nice to have you as my friend."

"I cherish the fact that you consider me a friend, Alana," Gordy replied. "And you're right: there probably are some who don't feel about you as I do. I'm sure that Bill Sterling wouldn't feel about you and your happiness in the way that I do.

"He and Miss I'm-going-to-be-a-star Starwalt are very likely enjoying themselves immensely right now. They're two of a kind, you know. And so, my darling, are we. You'll see when we get to know one another even better. I'm going to ask Mother if she'll have you over to dinner."

"We'll see," Alana said, careful not to commit herself.

As quickly as Gordy wanted to move into her life, she felt a sense of alarm. Already he was getting grandiose ideas, and she wondered how to discourage him without hurting his feelings.

"I know you've been spending time with Bill Sterling, but I've seen his type, my dear. No doubt he's a cad and a rake. A heartbreaker for sure. But I? Should you allow it, I would live only to take care of you and make you happy."

"Surely you've more to do than concern yourself with my doings," Alana chided.

Gordy did admit to the volunteer activities in which he took part and the social extravaganzas. Without bragging, he sketched in the fact that he didn't have to work because he lived off the dividends produced by long dead ancestors' farsighted labors.

"So at the moment I'm more than free to make your happiness my number one priority. When you are happy, my darling girl, I am happy. And when I am happy, Mother is, too."

twelve

The next day, Alana was surprised when Gloria Sheffield-Walters, Gordy's mother, came into the boutique. Mrs. Sheffield-Walters greeted Alana warmly, then immediately launched into the reason behind her unexpected visit.

"Gordon has told me how much he's enjoyed your company at the musical rehearsals," she said. "I appreciate the attention and affection you've given my boy, and I'd like to get to know you better. We're having a small dinner party a week from this Saturday night. We'd love nothing better, my dear, than to be able to count you among the charming guests who'll be invited. Are you free? I realize that it's rather short notice."

"Well—"

"Oh heavens!" the woman cried, not waiting for Alana to answer before she approached a sale rack, like a ship under full steam. "What darling little trinkets! These will make superb favors for our guests at the dinner party. Have you enough in supply so that I could purchase twenty-four?" she asked, holding the item aloft.

"Yes, I think so," Alana said, realizing what such a sale would do for their day's proceeds. "Let me check."

Quickly she went into the stockroom and returned with a box.

"You're in luck. Counting those on display we have exactly twenty-four."

"How wonderful!" Mrs. Sheffield-Walters trilled, reaching into her designer handbag for a charge card. "Now, about that dinner party—are you free?"

"Yes," Alana said. "I accept your kind invitation with pleasure."

"Magnificent! Gordon will be *so* happy. He's adored you from afar for a long, long time. There have been any number of girls who've thrown themselves at him. Gold-digging types. You're not that kind. As his mother it reassures me that you're attracted to my boy for honest and aboveboard reasons."

Carrie came in just then, and Alana introduced the two women. Carrie was sweet and cordial, but Mrs. Sheffield-Walters seemed to be looking down her aristocratic nose, viewing Carrie as a common shop girl. Alana sensed her friend bristle over the attitude.

The brass bell from the Orient that hung over the door had scarcely ceased its merry sound after Mrs. Sheffield-Walters left, when Carrie gave a snort.

"Well, la-di-dah!" she said, folding her arms defensively across her chest.

"She's quite a pattern, isn't she?" Alana asked, amused. "But when you get to know her, she's nice, in a socially privileged kind of way. Her son, Gordon, is a friend of mine."

"Born with a silver spoon in his mouth?" Carrie questioned.

Alana nodded. "It would appear so."

"Well, I'll take those who use stainless steel silverware any day of the week!"

"I'll be dining off real silverware a week from this Saturday night," Alana said. "Mrs. Sheffield-Walters just bopped in to invite me to a dinner party. *And*," she added, hoping to assuage Carrie's ruffled feathers, "she just bought out our entire stock of those trinkets that I'd ordered and then wondered what on earth we were going to do with them since they seemed not to appeal to our average clientele."

"Well, thank the Lord for small miracles," Carrie said. "That's great. You're going?"

"Yes, for Gordon's sake," Alana said. "He's really very nice. Not at all like his mother, although to be honest, he does have his moments of being a bit superior."

Carrie gave a philosophical shrug. "When you've been raised in that kind of environment, I'm sure it's hard not to take on airs. We're all products of our upbringing," she added. "I'm so grateful that I was raised in a good, Christian home that stressed godly principles and values."

"Ummm...," Alana said, unwilling to get into a conversation in that area at the moment. "What do you think I should wear?"

"Alana, you'd be a knockout in a burlap bag."

Alana smiled. "That's how Gordy feels. But I want to look smashing. It's anyone's guess what important people will be attending. I don't want to embarrass them by being either over- or underdressed. Can you believe it? She invites me to a small dinner party. I'm thinking in terms of five or six people, and she purchases *two dozen* party favors."

"Small is in the eye of the beholder," Carrie said. "I guess it's all relative. I hope, though," she cautioned and seemed to grope carefully for her words, "that you're not going to find yourself in over your head."

"I'm a big girl," Alana pointed out.

"I know, but that wasn't what I meant."

"Well, believe it or not, even though sometimes I seem to exist on Big Macs and ordered-in pizza, I do know which fork to use—"

"Lannie, Lannie, would you please stop attempting to put words in my mouth?" Carrie interrupted in exasperation. "That's not what I meant. I'm sure you'll do just fine on that score. It's simply that I have this feeling of unease about Gordon Walters. It's silly, I know, but there seems to be something that I really should remember, but just can't seem to recall. You're sure he's an okay kind of guy?"

"Positive," Alana assured, and described in great detail

exactly what sort of person Gordy Walters was.

"That's a relief," Carrie said. "He does sound very nice. I have to be honest, I suppose the only reason I find myself feeling less than enthusiastic about Gordy walking into your life and taking over the front-and-center position is because I've seen you with Bill Sterling long enough that I'd begun to think of you as a couple."

"I think Bill did, too," Alana admitted, suddenly willing to be frank herself. "And I'll admit that fact added to the attraction of an involvement with Gordon. If nothing else, it proves to Bill that he's not free to make any assumptions about anything."

"He knows that you're seeing Gordy?" Carrie asked.

"He should, but that doesn't mean he does," Alana replied. "He's been keeping such steady company with Missy Starwalt that perhaps he hasn't even noticed."

"Is *that* her name?" Carrie gasped, then she blushed when she realized that she'd spoken in a rash manner.

"Whose name? Then you've seen them together?"

Carrie nodded. "Bill brought her to church last Sunday morning. You didn't see her because you weren't at services with us. Mark and I were both wondering who she was. But Bill didn't linger long enough to have to make introductions."

"Maybe he's not proud enough of her to want to introduce her to his friends," Alana blurted out before she could stop herself, even though she realized how judgmental, uncharitable, even jealous the words sounded.

"It could be," Carrie said, "although we have to remember that there was no one so high and mighty that Jesus wouldn't seek that person out, and there was no one so down and out that our Lord wouldn't sit down and fellowship with them. Jesus didn't come to heal the spiritually healthy. Jesus came to minister to and save the sinners who needed him."

"I'm sure you're right," Alana said. "Now, about my buying trip, can you spare me from the store early in March? I've tentatively pencilled in the dates on our calendar."

Carrie nodded. "We can make arrangements. It'll be no problem if we plan for it. But isn't that when *Oklahoma!* opens? Did you forget that? Don't you need to be here then?"

"That is when *Oklahoma!* opens," Alana admitted. "And it's no problem for me to be away. Missy Starwalt will perform as beautifully as Bill's leading lady in the community theater production as she apparently does in Bill's private life!"

"Alana Charles, if I didn't know better, I'd think you were jealous!" Carrie gasped.

Alana gave her a withering look. "Surely you jest," she said, giving a wry laugh. "It's of no concern to me what Bill Sterling does—or with whom he does it," she added in a firm tone, hoping that if she offered that sentiment enough times and to enough people, the knowledge would make its way from her head to her heart. Maybe then she would be free of the unsettling effect Bill Sterling, and his influence, seemed to hold over the life she led.

thirteen

The dinner party at Gloria Sheffield-Walters's home was an unqualified success. Alana had faced it with some trepidation, but once there she had a wonderful time. Gordon was a debonair and attentive suitor, and the way his mother's friends beamed at Alana, she felt their social circle gave its approval to the relationship.

Everyone made a great fuss over the favors, and when Gloria admitted to locating them at Alana's shop, several of the women present inquired if she had business cards with her. She passed them out, receiving promises that Gloria and Gordon's friends would be stopping by to pay her a visit at the Shoestring Boutique.

The party was so much fun that Alana didn't depart as early as she had intended. She was late enough getting home that the next morning, promise or no, she phoned Carrie to beg off about attending church services.

She truly did have a sore throat when she called to alert her friend not to bother to swing by to pick her up. But she also had a sore heart, and she didn't wish to be trying to focus on the pastor's message while across the aisle Bill Sterling would likely be sitting with Missy Starwalt.

Alana had become so accustomed to going to services that when she missed attending, oddly enough, her life felt out of kilter, as if somehow direction were lacking.

Sunday seemed overly long, although Gordon called that afternoon to chat for a while. Instead of moping and giving in to the lethargy and poor spirits that threatened to overtake her, Alana used the opportunity to get caught up on a few tasks she had been meaning to attend to for a long time.

On Monday, she heard nothing from Gordon—or Bill—all day, and she found it a welcome respite, for it allowed her to single-mindedly attend to work at the boutique without time-consuming interruptions or stressful feelings to siphon off her mental and physical energies.

She knew a pleasant sense of accomplishment when she prepared to go to the rehearsal that night. The opening night was only a few weeks away—as was her buying trip—and she was present at rehearsals, now serving as Melissa's understudy.

Gordon was late arriving at the auditorium. Alana was seated in the darkness. She cast him a smile as he dropped into the seat next to her. While she awaited the action, Gordon seemed fidgety, but Alana was scarcely aware of it when he excused himself to go to the restroom. A moment later he was back, still carefully and firmly wiping his hands on the paper towel that he tucked into his pocket.

"She's good," Alana murmured.

"Who?" Gordy inquired.

"Missy. She may be conceited and she may be full of herself, but the inarguable fact is that she is excellent as

Laurey. In fact, she's so good that I really don't see any need for me to return from my buying trip to take over. That truly makes more bother for everyone involved than if she had the starring role for the rest of the season. I think that after rehearsal, I'll tell the director how I feel."

Gordy placed a restraining hand on her arm.

"Bite your tongue, dear girl! I daresay that she wouldn't be so generous in your direction as you are in hers. There's no need to reach a hasty decision. There's always time to move on that idea if at a later time you choose to."

"I suppose you're right," Alana agreed, idly noting that her starring in the production seemed to mean more to Gordy than it did to her.

"Of course I am. No sense letting her have both the leading role and the boyfriend who jilted you for an involvement with her."

At the word "jilt," Alana's heart squeezed with pain from which she had long since believed she'd recovered.

"He didn't jilt me," she gasped.

"No. I'm aware that he didn't, my darling, for I was there when you accepted my invitation instead of his. If anyone was jilted in the affair, 'twas him."

"Knowing that, why are you even bringing up the matter?" Alana asked in a confrontational tone of voice.

"It's really not I bringing it up, my dear. But there are some things I think you should know. There are those who are talking about you, pitying you, as if you've been jilted by Bill. Perhaps he said something to salve her ego. Or perhaps it's merely Missy making such remarks to solidify her position. Whatever, it really doesn't matter. I only felt you should know the murmurings among some of the cast members."

"Well, if you hear further murmurings, Gordon, I would consider it a personal favor to me if you would set the record straight."

"Oh, I will," he promised. "With pleasure. But don't let it spoil our night, Alana. It's such an inconsequential matter. We can't trouble ourselves with the comments and actions of people like Missy and Bill. What goes around comes around. And like I've told you in the past, my darling, eventually that type pays for their transgressions. Surely Missy's day of reckoning is just around the corner. At least, if there's any fairness in this world, she will get exactly what she deserves!"

Alana gave a shudder as she realized Gordy actually seemed to be wishing misfortune on the gregarious, sometimes thoughtless, young woman.

"Surely you don't mean that, Gordon."

He gave a bland shrug.

"I've seen it happen enough times in life to believe in the concept. Not that I'm wishing ill upon her. Please understand. But that type seems to continually go through life making enemies. The way she's rankled people here within the community theater group, just imagine the kinds of enemies she's collected in her business or personal life."

"You're probably right."

"And you, my dear, are a refreshing change from our star

of the production. I should think you wouldn't have an enemy in the world," Gordon said, "but a great number of admirers. And I'm jealous of each and every one of them, although I do fancy myself your number one fan."

"You shouldn't be envious," Alana said.

Gordon turned to her with anxious eyes.

"Do I dare believe you mean what I would hope by that sentiment?"

Gordy had been so supportive to her and was so kind and decent that Alana couldn't withhold a dab of affection when it meant so much to him.

"You're special to me, Gordon. A friend unlike all others."

"Only a friend?" he inquired, his tone teasing, but at the same time a bit petulant.

"A friend, but with the potential to become much, much more."

"Then I shall wait for that happy day," he assured. "I'll wait forever if I must, and do whatever I must to ensure that one day you will be mine. All mine. My leading lady of love."

Then in the darkened auditorium, Gordy boldly draped his arm around Alana's shoulders and cast an arch look in the direction of those who took notice. He gave her arm a tender, secretive, possessive little squeeze.

"Are we on for coffee, dear?" Gordon inquired when the rehearsal ended.

"I really have a lot of things that I need to do at my apartment," Alana demurred, feeling unsettled by the turn things had taken. When given an inch, Gordon seemed to want to take a yard.

"Could I come up for a nightcap?"

Alana paused, as if giving it careful consideration.

"I really don't think so," she refused "although I'm touched that you want to spend time with me. I really do have pressing things to attend to. Please understand?"

"Of course," he agreed. "We all have our obligations." He quickly drew her hand into his, then brought her fingertips to his lips and gave them a quick kiss. "I'll be in touch," he promised, "and if not sooner, then I'll see you at rehearsal the night after next."

"I'll be looking forward to it," Alana replied.

No sooner did the words leave her lips than she realized that they were a lie. She no longer looked forward to time spent with Gordon. She felt overwhelmed by it. Suffocated. But he was so nice that she simply couldn't find it within herself to tell him how she felt, or why, when she didn't even understand it herself.

She had managed to discard Bill, and he'd immediately discovered an interest in Missy. Maybe, just maybe, she could get out of her sticky, confining relationship with Gordy by arranging for him to become romantically involved with someone else.

But who? She had two days to reflect on it. Perhaps come the next rehearsal, she would have her matchmaking figured out, and she could get an old love to forget about her by encouraging a relationship with a new love.

fourteen

After a busy day at the boutique because Carrie was out with the flu, Alana grabbed a sandwich at a fast-food, drive-up window, then rushed to get to the auditorium.

The lot was filled with cars, and she feared that she would be late as she rushed across the icy lot and let herself into the cavernous theater building. As she approached the auditorium, she heard an excited babble of voices. Instead of the cast members and stage crew being clustered in small knots, discussing various topics, they were all piled into one, gigantic huddle.

From the almost electric charge to the air surrounding them, Alana sensed that they were discussing a tragedy, not some key element regarding the successful staging of *Oklahoma!*

"Oh, it's absolutely terrible," she overheard one woman say.

"It-it's so upsetting. She's so young," another added.

"I wonder if...," another ventured, but then seemed not to have the will to finish the idea.

"I hope she doesn't die," said one of the younger women who was working as a prompter. "I've never known anyone who's died, and I don't want to start now."

"I'm sure she's getting the best care possible," another

reassured.

"Yes, and you must keep in mind that St. Louis is the medical center of the Midwest. If she can't get the care she needs here, she probably couldn't receive it anywhere else. I should know. I work at Barnes Hospital, and that's where she was taken. So at least put your minds to ease on that point."

"That's a relief," someone spoke up, sighing.

"I'll try to find out what I can," the nurse offered. "Since I'm on staff, I'm sure that the ICU nurses will speak more openly to me than they might if I were an outsider."

"What's wrong? What's happened?" Alana whispered. A chill of alarm passed through her. She glanced worriedly from one face to another.

"It's Missy," the director explained. "She was involved in a terrible accident the night before last following rehearsal."

"Oh, no!" Alana exclaimed. "What happened?"

"She ran a red light and was broadsided by a semi."

Alana winced. She could all too easily envision the scene. From remarks Missy had made, Alana suspected that the girl drove a bit fast and recklessly. Many people felt that the yellow light, instead of meaning caution, meant to hit the gas in order to squeak through the intersection before the light changed to red. Missy drove a tiny compact car that got excellent mileage but wouldn't afford much protection against an eighteen-wheeler hauling a full load of freight.

"Is she going to be all right?" Alana inquired.

"The doctors are optimistic," the director said. "Her mother told me that she's still in a coma but that the doctors believe she'll be conscious soon. She's still in critical condition, but if her condition remains stable through tomorrow, they believe the medical crisis will have passed and that it's pretty well assured that she'll be out of the woods."

"How dreadful," Gordon said, clucking, as he sadly shook his head over the news. "I heard about the accident on the news, but the name didn't register. I figured that it was someone else with the same name."

"I know. That's what happened to me, too," the man who played Jud Fry said. "I guess you figure that it won't happen to you—and that it won't happen to your friends, either."

"If I'd have known it was Missy," Gordon said, "I'd have ordered flowers delivered to the hospital."

"Really, we should," someone else agreed.

"Count me in."

"Me, too."

"Gordy, since you brought it up, would you mind ordering flowers from all of us? We could repay you."

He gave a gentle nod. "Consider it done. Any special selection you'd like? Or message on the card?"

The women concurred that an arrangement of pink tea roses would be nice and not so terribly large that it would get in the way of the nursing staff.

"As for the message, we'll leave that up to you, Gordy. You'll know what's appropriate."

"Very well. I'll attend to it right away."

"We'd better get down to business," the director said. "Mrs. Starwalt said that Missy will have a long and difficult recuperation. She broke her jaw. She won't be singing for a long, long time, if ever. So she won't be our leading lady on opening night." The director gave a careful pause. "Alana? Can you take center stage again, if you please?"

"Do it, darling!" Gordy uttered under his breath. "You'll be wonderful."

"Well," Alana said hesitantly.

She thought about her needed trip, but remembered that she had not booked her non-refundable airline tickets. She could cancel the hotel reservations, alter her plans, and take part in the musical with very little inconvenience.

The thought was cinched when she glanced toward Bill and saw the look in his eyes. He was almost pleading with her to join him center stage, and she realized that he wanted her there, more than ever, playing opposite him.

He had warned her that he would do anything to win her back. Did that include...? No! She wouldn't allow herself to think such a thing. It was an accident. The director had said so. And that was that.

Alana took her place on stage, and although she felt a bit rusty, soon she was moving into the play with verve and vitality. There was a special chemistry between Bill and Alana that caused the other members of the cast to catch the fire of enthusiasm. Gordy wasn't the only one who was a vocal fan after rehearsal ended.

"You're going to be stupendous on opening night, darling girl," Gordy assured. "And what an audience you'll play for. Mother's friends are going to turn out in force. It will be a powerful and important assemblage. It's a tragic thing that happened to Missy, poor girl, but perhaps it will work out for the best."

Alana realized that several cast members gave him unbelieving glances, as if they couldn't comprehend a remark so gauche when Missy's life still hung by a thread, but Alana knew Gordy didn't mean what he said.

"Are we on for coffee, Alana?" Gordy asked.

"Well, I do have things I need to do."

"Just a quick cup?" he tempted.

Alana nodded.

"Okay. But only one," she murmured. "I guess I need to unwind a bit before I go home to be alone with my thoughts."

"A penny for your thoughts," Gordy bribed.

Alana gave a low chuckle.

"I'm afraid that they're worth a quarter, at least."

"Then two bits it is," he said, playfully reaching into his pocket.

"Sorry. No deal," Alana said. "Some things are better left unsaid."

"And some things are better spoken honestly, especially if from the heart. There's something I need to say, Alana darling," Gordy whispered. His breath steamed the air as they stood outside her locked car in the parking lot.

"I love you. I've never felt about another woman as I feel

about you. I worship you. I adore you. I am absolutely, positively obsessed with you—"

"Gordon, that's truly sweet, but...." Further words failed Alana. She felt a chill. She'd only wanted to be Gordon's friend, but obviously he felt about her in a way vastly different from how she regarded him.

She had intended to keep his company only long enough to discourage Bill. Now she realized that she had bailed out of one sticky situation only to land smack dab in the middle of a worse one.

"Don't you love me, too? At least a little bit?" Gordon coaxed.

"Well, I'm very fond of you," Alana said. "And I like you quite well."

"But you don't love me?" he asked, his tone hurt.

"Gordy, I don't know what I feel."

"Very well. You don't love me right now. But do you think that, given time and encouragement, you could learn to love me?"

Silence spun between them. Alana had the sensation that her answer was very important.

"Anything is possible."

"And this will not only be possible, my darling, but it will become a reality."

Then, without asking permission, Gordy swept Alana into his arms, and his winter-chilled cheeks collided with hers as his warm lips sought hers in a possessive kiss. She allowed it for only a split second before she gracefully escaped from his embrace.

"This is for you, sweetheart," Gordy said. "It's a few days early, but I just can't wait until Valentine's Day." He pressed a small, beautifully wrapped package into her hand.

"Thank you very much," Alana said nervously. "It's very thoughtful of you. Now I've really got to go, Gordy. I just remembered some book work that I have to get done for an appointment with our accountant to do our tax return. I can't take time for coffee. I'm sorry."

"Can I call you tomorrow?"

"Of course," Alana curtly agreed. But then she quickly unlocked her car, started the engine, and sped away, pulse racing.

"Why, oh why, does life have to be so difficult and confusing," she lamented, as she banged the leather-covered steering wheel in miserable frustration.

She was so enmeshed in thought that only a split second before she would have run a red light did she collect her wits, slam on the recently repaired brakes, and skid to a halt inches before traffic surged from the other direction.

"When the play finishes running," she whispered, "I am going to go on a buying trip and maybe even take a long, long vacation. By then I will definitely need it."

People could assume that it was a well-deserved respite from work. But Alana knew the truth. It would be a desperate hiatus as she fled from relationships and the two men who both claimed to love her.

Alana, who had hastily unwrapped the small gift box as she waited at various red lights, discovered a diamond and ruby, heart-shaped pendant inside a velvet-covered, satin-lined case. As a retailer, she knew the real thing when she saw it, and she whistled low when she considered what it would cost even wholesale. It was much, much too expensive a gift to receive from Gordon unless he was deadly serious about one day making her his wife.

She didn't know what to do. Propriety demanded that she give it back, but Alana wasn't sure how Gordon would react. She was still upset when she returned home. She watched the evening news and was about to retire for the night when her telephone rang.

Almost no one had called her at that late hour in a long, long time. She felt a tremor of fear. She let the machine answer, but when she discovered Bill on the line she picked up the receiver.

"Still screening?" he inquired.

"Not really," she said. "So what's up?"

"Lannie, I'd really like to see you. Can I come up to your place? I know it's late. But I want to talk to you. In private," he added, his words seeming to attempt to convey a hidden meaning. "Are you alone?"

"Yes."

"Good. So can I come up?"

"I'll be waiting."

"Thanks, Pet. I appreciate it."

Alana flitted around the apartment, hastily bringing order to what was already her painstakingly neat residence. Periodically she glanced down to the street below, awaiting Bill's arrival, but she never did see his car pull up front. She was surprised when her doorbell chimed. Not sure that it was Bill, she opened the peephole and checked to make certain of her visitor's identity before she undid the series of locks to let him into her apartment.

"Bill, come in. Would you like some tea, coffee, fruit juice, or a soft drink?"

"A diet cola if you have it."

"Coming right up," Alana said, and entered the kitchenette. "What was it you wanted to see me about?" she prompted.

"I'm concerned about Missy."

"Of course you are," Alana said. "We all are. And I gather you've been seeing quite a lot of her."

"Then you gather wrong. Except for play practice, I've seen no more of her than I have of you. Oh, I take that back. We did have that one coffee date that she hornswoggled me into, and she was aware of what church I attended so, lo and behold when I arrived for services, she was waiting near the door. It would have been rude not to have sat with her."

"Oh. Then apparently I was mistaken," Alana said in a light voice, and hoped that the fact that her heart suddenly drummed to a calypso beat was not evidenced in her breathless tone.

"I went to the location where Missy's wrecked car is stored. I talked to the mechanic, and I looked it over myself. Please keep what I'm telling you in confidence. But it was no accident. Missy didn't run a red light because she's a young, reckless speed demon. Missy careened into that intersection because she had no brakes."

"No brakes?"

"The hose was cut. She lost all her brake fluid right after she left the theater parking lot."

"How awful," Alana said.

"I know that you didn't know her well, either," Bill said. "But I thought I'd start my private and personal investigation with you. Have you any idea of anyone who'd want to harm her."

Alana was dazed. "I haven't the foggiest idea," she admitted. "Except for our contact at the theater, we really do not know each other. I know nothing about her. I think she came into the boutique once or twice, but I think our items are a bit out of her price range."

Bill nodded. "Can you think of anyone that she's been close to at the theater?"

"Not really. She seemed as close to you as to anyone."

"And I scarcely knew the girl. Being with her wasn't a matter of holding an intelligent conversation, it was more like listening to a self-centered child prattle on about herself. I realized when she showed up at church that it wasn't out of an interest in getting to know the Lord. I think she merely wanted to get to know me better and was intent upon throwing herself in my path enough times for me to notice her."

"She can't be faulted for that," Alana said in a light tone. "There are probably many women at church who find their thoughts turning toward you when services are over."

"Ah, and were but that you were one of them," Bill

murmured.

"Perhaps you should go to Missy's place of employment and talk to her co-workers," Alana suggested. "That could be illuminating. Several weeks ago, Gordy commented that he felt that Missy was the type to make enemies everywhere she went. He believed her self-centered and egotistical. He really didn't like her."

"I gather that he certainly likes you."

"More than I'd like."

"Is he bothering you?" Bill asked, and gave Alana a dark glance that seemed to signal he was intent on protecting her with his life if need be.

Alana smiled.

"Nothing like that, Bill. He's been every bit the gentleman. It appears he's smitten. He's serious and I'm not. I don't know how to do anything but hurt him when I make it clear that I can't give him what he feels will make him happy."

"Having you back in the leading role seemed to make his day," Bill said.

"It certainly did," Alana agreed. "It was almost embarrassing the way he was so elated over it. It seemed so tactless and bizarre for Gordy to be so openly overjoyed that I was playing Laurey again when poor Missy is lying in the ICU with tubes running in, tubes running out, and doctors unsure if she'll even live or not."

"How well do you know this Gordon fellow?" Bill asked.

"What do you mean?"

"Just what I said."

"Well enough," Alana said, shrugging. She sketched in what she had learned of the family when she had dined with his widowed mother and their friends. "He's certainly respectable enough."

"Is he reputable?"

"Why wouldn't he be? Bill, I know you. Just what are you driving at?"

He sighed.

"Pet, at the risk of offending you, I'll be brutally honest. Do you think that Gordy could have had anything to do with Missy's accident?"

Alana's mouth dropped open in shock. "How can you think such a thing?" she gasped. "Granted, Gordy Walters is different. He's eccentric. He's not easily understood by other people. But I doubt that he's a psychotic, would-be murderer."

"Okay. But I had to ask. You were with him that night. I figured that you'd be aware if there'd been any absences. Logic dictates that it was done in the auditorium's parking lot, or Missy'd have had trouble with her brakes before she arrived. That does point the finger of suspicion at someone in the group."

"I hadn't thought of that," Alana murmured, horrified.

"If it was a random incident by a neighborhood vandal, why Missy's car? Why only her car?"

"I see what you mean," Alana said.

"It's really not my business to investigate. But I'm making it my concern," Bill said. "The past being what it is, I feel that I owe you that much."

"Owe me?" Alana questioned, puzzled.

"I may as well tell you right now, Alana. People are talking. You're the one that they suspect."

"Me?" she gasped, horrified and alarmed. "Why on earth would they suspect me?"

"Why wouldn't they?" Bill retorted, but didn't wait for her to answer. "You were suddenly bumped from the leading role, and Missy was given a chance to be a star. With her brake line cut and a serious accident that totaled out her car, voila! Suddenly you are the leading lady again."

"Oh, how awful. Bill, that's not what happened. I swear it's not. And the director can back me up."

"I think you'd better start talking, Lannie. Tell me everything. Be honest with me. No matter how it makes you look."

"I didn't do it, Bill," Alana stated firmly and proceeded to explain about her business trip.

"I believe you. Do you think that it's possible Gordy did?"

"Anything's possible," she admitted. She squirmed for a long moment. "I guess I should mention this, although I feel like such a betrayer. Gordy was about ten minutes late arriving, and you know how prompt he is. He's usually one of the first to arrive.

"He sat by me, but he was fidgety, and then he went to the restroom. When he came back I could smell the soap from the dispenser. He sat down and continued to dry his hands with the paper towel. And...," Alana paused, reluctant.

"Yes? Go on."

"He wasn't so much drying his hands, Bill, as it seemed he was wiping them."

"Ah. As if to rub away grease or grime."

"Exactly," Alana said, sighing heavily.

"Maybe Gordon is our man," Bill said. "Until we know, please be careful."

"I will."

"I guess I'd better be going," Bill said.

Just then, Alana's doorbell rang. She shuddered with alarm. She was suddenly glad that Bill was there for protection. She put on a brave front and casually walked to the door. She felt silly and almost weak with relief when she discovered her next door neighbor, an abashed look on her face, asking for a pain reliever.

"Sure. Just a minute," Alana said and went to her medicine cabinet.

Alana chatted with her neighbor for just a moment. When she reentered her apartment, Bill had put on his coat and gloves and was standing near the window overlooking the street.

"I'll be going now, Alana. Thanks for your help. And I think that you should keep it between us that we had this conversation."

"I will," Alana said.

Instead of kissing her good night, Bill merely patted her shoulder, murmured, "Good night," and then strode toward the elevator.

A few minutes later, Alana looked out onto the street. She saw Bill's car parked where he had hidden it when she had complained to Carrie that she was under surveillance. This time, instead of feeling angry about it, she sensed comfort in knowing that her PI ex-fiancé cared enough to watch over her the way he believed the Lord looked after him.

His car was still there when she went to bed, but it was gone when she arose with the first rays of the morning sun.

fifteen

That day at work, Alana tried to block out the disturbing information Bill had given her and his equally disturbing theories. She called the nurse who was part of the theater group and was relieved to learn that Missy was going to be all right.

Alana had just arrived home and was preparing to depart for the theater when her home phone rang. She scooped up the receiver without even thinking to screen.

"Lannie? Bill. I was wondering if you could do me a huge favor and give me a lift to the theater."

"Sure thing."

"Sorry to impose, but my car is still in the shop. It'll soon be two weeks I've been making do with cabs and rides from friends."

"It's what?"

"In the shop. I'm having some body work done, and it's taken them longer than expected. They've got a replacement part on order and it's coming from overseas."

But Bill's car had been parked in the street, hadn't it?

"How did you get to my apartment last night when you came over and we talked about Missy's accident?"

"A taxi, of course, Lannie. The same way I left."

"Oh." Suddenly Alana felt bleak. It was a topic she knew

150

that she didn't want to pursue. At least not yet.

When she hung up she looked at her telephone. She realized she had not made any calls from her home telephone since Bill had left the night before. Taking a deep breath, wondering if she would find proof that Bill was a liar, she pressed the redial button.

"Metro-East Cab Company," a woman dispatcher replied.

"Sorry. Wrong number," Alana said and hung up.

Bill was telling the truth. That meant that it was not he who was keeping watch on her. But if it was not Bill, who in the world could it be? And why on earth would the person want to do it?

Thirty minutes later Alana retrieved Bill outside his apartment building. As she drove, she kept a critical eye on the traffic around her. When she parked in the lot she activated the security alarms on her car.

"Remember, Pet, be very careful what you say. We don't want to alert anyone to our suspicions that someone in the theater group is guilty of wrongdoing. And we also don't want to offer false witness against someone who might very well be innocent."

"Gotcha," she glumly agreed.

That night their performance was a bit off, but others apparently didn't notice. There was less enthusiastic applause from the audience, for Gordon, who'd become a regular, was absent that evening.

"Can I interest you in a cup of coffee?" Bill asked.

"I'd been planning on asking you if you didn't invite

me," Alana said, smiling.

"The regular place? The one you've been going to with Gordon?"

"No. I'd like to go someplace new."

"I know just the place," Bill said.

Alana handed him the keys to her car.

"You drive, okay?"

"Your wish is my desire, milady."

Alana gave a weak smile and realized that it was true. At the moment, Bill seemed so trustworthy. Why, oh, why, couldn't she believe that he would always be like this?

Bill and Alana had a lovely conversation over coffee and danish at a small coffee shop that served out-of-this-world pastries. She felt her heart warming toward him, but his manner chilled as they got ready to leave. Something had changed his attitude, and Alana felt a sense of acute frustration. So many times when she felt as if she was at long last getting to know—and like—the real Bill Sterling, he changed on her like a chameleon.

"Rather than driving to my apartment, Alana, I'm going to see you safely home," he said in a way that brooked no argument. "I'll take a cab from your place to mine."

"Very well," Alana said.

When Bill parked in Alana's assigned slot, he faced her.

"I'm going to come up and check out your apartment."

"Bill—"

"It's better to be safe than sorry," he said.

"What's going on?" Alana asked in a voice made thin with anxiety.

"I don't know," Bill admitted. "But I'm most certainly going to find out. And until I do, we're taking no chances that your understudy is going to get a chance to be the leading lady on opening night."

Nervous apprehension drove Alana to silence as Bill went through her apartment.

"The coast is clear," he reported.

Then, almost pointedly, Bill walked to her picture window. He glanced up and down the street, as did Alana. There was the car, the car that she had believed was Bill's, but couldn't be. Who had a car identical to Bill's foreign luxury sports car except for the number on the license plate? No one that she knew.

Was Bill's car really in the shop? Or did he just say it was there so that he could have an associate park his car outside her apartment, convincing Alana that someone else wished her harm.

Suddenly Alana realized that Bill Sterling could have set her up to swallow a huge set of lies. He might be portraying himself as her protector, terrifying her back into his life, and frightening her away from poor Gordy Walters.

Alana's head was swirling when she went to bed. It took an act of will to convince herself to stop thinking about it. A short time later, she fell into deep and dreamless sleep.

sixteen

Alana was on pins and needles for the next few days, but things were peaceful. She hoped she wasn't experiencing the lull before the storm.

Early Sunday morning she received two crank calls. She had promised Mark and Carrie that she would attend church services with them, and she found herself looking forward to attending if only to escape the confines of her apartment.

Earlier in the week Carrie had told her the pastor's plans for the weekend worship services, and Alana had looked up the Scripture in an old Bible of hers that she had dug out from a box in her closet. Increasingly she realized that many of God's children had gone through times when they felt abandoned by Him. But their feelings and the difficult circumstances they faced didn't change God's love for them.

After morning worship, the three friends found Bill waiting for them at the end of their pew.

"If you're all free, I'd like to take you out to dinner today," Bill said. He looked to Mark. "It seems the least I can do to repay your kindness in giving me a lift to the office each morning."

Mark glanced toward where Bill's gleaming car was

parked.

"Lookin' good!" he said, making a thumbs up sign.

Bill gave it an assessing glance.

"Worth the wait," he said, smiling. "Some things are."
He gave Alana a pointed look. She was caught off guard,
and her tongue shifted into gear before her mind could
follow suit.

"Then it is true—"

"What's true?" Bill asked.

"Nothing," Alana said, flushing. "I'm sorry if I'm not
making sense. I had my mind on something else."

"Where would you like to eat?" Bill asked, changing the
subject. The friends discussed their options and decided on
a place.

"Why don't you ride with me, Alana?" Bill cordially
invited.

Alana was about to find a way to politely refuse, but she
realized there was no way to do so, especially with Carrie
almost shoving her in Bill's direction.

"Okay," she said, reluctantly agreeing.

Once they were in the car, Bill turned to her and gave a
crooked smile.

"You don't have to seem so overjoyed to be in my
company," he chided, chucking her on the chin, forcing
her bleak face to confront his. She tried to smile, but
instead, her eyes tingled with wetness that gave them the
sheen of unshed tears.

"Please, Bill."

"Lannie, what's wrong?" he asked, concerned.

"Nothing. Everything. Oh, I don't know! I'm just so confused. So terribly, terribly confused."

"About what?"

"I don't know. No, I do know, but it's just that I can't talk about it—"

"Can't? Or won't?"

Alana's temper rose as the memory of her problems brought back the tremendous fear she had been experiencing.

"Can't? Won't? Take your pick—but leave me alone about it."

And Bill did.

At the restaurant, Carrie and Alana went to the powder room. As Carrie was tracing on lipstick, her eyes met Alana's in the mirror.

"Hey, about not making any sense, old pal, who do you think you were fooling? What were you really talking about?"

"Nothing."

"Don't give me that. Perhaps you took in Mark and Bill, but not me. What's on your mind?"

"Oh, nothing really. It's just that Bill told me that his car was in the shop is all," Alana admitted. "And for some rather private reasons and, I'll admit, due to what now looks like false evidence, I didn't believe him. It was rather nice to learn that he was telling the truth. At least this time...or let's say I hope he is."

Alana's thoughts spun back to intricate situations in the past when Bill had spared no energy to make a situation appear to be what it was not. As a consequence, casual onlookers would believe the lie was the unvarnished truth and view the truth as the most outrageous fabrication.

"I think Bill Sterling tells the truth all the time," Carrie said. "I've never caught him in a lie. I'm sure Mark hasn't either."

"Perhaps you haven't known him long enough," Alana casually challenged, shrugging as she fluffed her hair, trying to present such disinterest that Carrie wouldn't realize just how troubled she was.

"Perhaps you no longer know him well enough," Carrie said, unable or unwilling to drop the subject. "Bill is a changed man, made new, reborn in the Lord. But I guess until you've learned to trust the Lord again, you won't be able to trust Bill Sterling.

Alana felt uncomfortable, fearful that Carrie was going to begin urging her toward a more vocal and visible commitment to the Lord. There were times during church services when Alana felt very much at one with the others in the congregation. But other times, she held back.

Surrounded by believers, she felt a barrier. They so easily trusted God and enjoyed such feelings of security and protection. She hadn't known what that was like since her parents had died, and she wasn't sure if she would ever again experience that peace.

"Let's just drop it, okay? I have a headache. It has been a lousy week, and I'd really rather not fight—especially with a friend."

"Okay," Carrie answered, uncertainty coloring her words.

"Let's declare a truce and go enjoy a lovely meal and excellent company. Not another word will be said— today."

During the lavish and beautifully prepared meal, Alana found herself being polite but silent. Bill was doing his best to put on a commendable performance as a congenial host. Even so she realized he was as uncomfortable over dinner as she. Carrie and Mark, wrapped in bliss, seemed oblivious to the tensions between their two friends.

Alana, hoping that Mark and Carrie would give her a ride home, was disappointed when they seemed to think that Alana and Bill in the same car was, if not perfection, at least a step in the right direction. They explained that they had things they needed to attend to and hinted that it would be a wonderful favor if Bill could take Alana.

Bill was quick on the uptake, so much so that Alana wondered if the entire morning had been a carefully acted out skit, with Carrie and Mark willing performers in the mini-drama.

"I'll see Alana home," Bill said, when Mark and Carrie had set the stage for such a natural offer.

"Great!" Mark answered, so quickly and enthusiastically that Alana felt miffed. She was casting about for a way to extricate herself with the firm and inarguable idea that she would call a taxi and see herself home, but there seemed no way to change things with Bill's firm grip on her arm leading her toward his car.

Carrie and Mark waved cheerfully as they pulled out of the parking lot. Bill paused a moment before he started his car.

"Is there anything you'd like to do? If you have the afternoon free and would like to do something, I'm available, and your wish is my command."

"No." Alana's tone was glum, and she pointedly adjusted herself on the leather seat of Bill's car, carefully guarding her own space.

"Nothing except go straight home?" he asked as he slid on kidskin leather driving gloves.

"Yes." Alana noticed how rigid and unfriendly the syllable sounded, but she was too piqued at the three of them to care. Silence spiraled between them. It was broken by a desolate sigh and Bill's soft, hurt tone.

"Why do you still hate me?"

Prickly silence stretched between them, begging to be broken, but it was a few minutes before Alana was able to respond.

"I don't hate you," she said tightly, her eyes sparking defensively. She felt angry that he had the ability and the opportunity to force a confrontation between them.

"What *do* you feel?"

Alana took a quick mental inventory and realized that she didn't know what she was feeling. She was surrounded by swirls of emotions and didn't recognize them except to know that they seemed basically unpleasant. She didn't like dealing with them and resented Bill forcing her to against her will.

"I don't feel anything," she finally said in a bleak tone. "Nothing."

Bill groaned with exasperation.

"Come on, Alana, get honest. If you felt nothing, you'd be able to treat me better than you do. I've heard it said that to hate you've generally once first loved. Sometimes you're nice, and I get my hopes up. Other times you're so distant and cold I feel as if I'm in danger of catching pneumonia. Those swings in mood make me realize that you have a lot of feelings. I don't know just what they are. Perhaps you don't know."

Alana gave him a steely look.

"How do you expect me to act?" she asked in a sharp, testy tone.

"Maybe that's my error," he said, instead of replying to her question. He nodded as if suddenly everything had a richer, deeper meaning, and that instead of it being her problem, it was actually his own issue.

"I guess I did have my expectations. If I had expected nothing, then I wouldn't be disappointed, would I?" His tone was level, laced with logic and acceptance.

"You have no right to expect anything from me, Bill. Not after what you did!" Alana said, unable to contain the rage that had been building in her.

"Are you going to go to your grave hating me? Are you going to hold me unforgiven with your dying breath?" Bill asked, and suddenly there was fire in his eyes. The fire of passion. The fire of fervor for his faith. And the fire of fear for her safety.

"There are no guarantees in this life, Pet. You know what Scripture says about forgiveness. Think of the Lord's

Prayer, for that matter, which you recited along with everyone else this morning." Bill paused. "Perhaps you believe you can punish me by refusing to forgive me. And if you refuse to do so, that is your right.

"But I know a thing or two about anger myself. I know that you've got to admit that anger. You've got to feel that anger instead of pushing it down and ignoring it and trying to pretend that it isn't there. Only when you're able to admit that you feel anger can you start grieving over what hurt you.

"Once you grieve over what's made you angry, you can move into the phase of forgiveness when you start to look beyond yourself and see that the parties involved never own the entire problem. It does take two people to tangle. I made my mistakes, and you, my dear, made a few mistakes, too.

"I'm trying to clean up my side of the street. You don't seem to have any interest in sweeping off your half of the path, and I won't attempt to do it for you—you own that side of the street. But I would like to tell you that in the past as I've worked through the stages—from anger, to grief, to forgiveness, to acceptance, to trying to live life as the Lord would have me—the rest of my life is going to be as serene and peaceful as possible in this world."

"Are you quite through?" Alana asked in a chilly voice. She felt her own errors in living were minuscule compared to the major damage Bill had done. Even so, his words were like salt in her wounds because in the dark soul of the night sometimes she did reflect on times when she had injured people.

But she always pushed those feelings away. As if she were adding up game score totals, she worked to find ways to adjust the scores so that she was always the party who had been wronged the most.

"The only one you really hurt by not forgiving others is yourself," Bill's voice interrupted Alana's thoughts. "I have assurance that the Lord has forgiven me every error I've made in life. It's too bad that I can't say the same about the woman I love as I've never loved another, but when the Lord chooses to convict you, He'll get the job done."

"My only conviction at the moment is a sincere wish that you'd shut up and leave me alone!" Alana fumbled in her handbag, snatched out a tissue, and swiped at the quick tears of hurt and fury that had spilled over and were rolling toward her trembling lips.

Bill sighed and pulled at his hair, revealing how upset he was.

"Yes. I am quite finished. And once again, I'm sorry," he said. "I owe you an apology. I have no right to make your spiritual state my business. No right except that, like it or not, Alana, I love you. Because of my love for God, I want the best for others, and I want you to know the Lord like I do. I even want miserable human beings, like the one who tampered with Missy's car and the one who seems to be watching you, to find the Lord and know healing from such sicknesses of the soul—"

"Why is it that no one will leave me alone?" Alana cried. "Why does everyone feel that they must push me to make a deep commitment to God that I don't feel and am not sure I want?"

"I'm sorry, Lannie. I didn't realize how touchy you are. I won't say another word. I'll take you right home. But I do want you to at least let me see you safely to your apartment. I insist. If you refuse me entrance, I will pay a call on your building's security officer and take him into my confidence. Then you'll risk having everyone know that something is up."

"Something is not up!" Alana hissed, struggling to push down the alarm.

"Hopefully, not. But the car—that car—is parked there again."

Even as he said it, Bill was reaching into his coat pocket for a tiny, voice-activated recorder. As they went by the parked vehicle, he spoke the tag number into the recorder and as a backup, scribbled it in a notebook.

"I'll call a well-placed friend who can get me the name in which the car is registered, even though it's Sunday," he explained. "I saw the car the other night when I was in the cab, but I didn't want to alert the person sitting in it that anyone was suspicious. The tag was obliterated by snow and ice and dirt that had sprayed up from the road."

Alana's heart lurched. Her face flushed hot as she realized how unreasonable she'd been and how patient Bill was. He truly seemed to have only her safety and best interests at heart, even though she was sometimes rude and hostile and let him know by word and attitude that she trusted him less than any other person on earth.

Suddenly, frightened though she was, Alana was filled with relief that a man like Bill was at her side wanting to protect her. Or was he? It was possible that Bill had been watching her and that he had had one of his investigators pick up an identical car from a rental agency to throw off her suspicions. Maybe Bill thought that by making her believe he couldn't possibly have been watching her when she was with him in his car, she would learn to trust him.

She decided that the best way to handle the situation was to act as if she believed his story. Maybe if he let down his guard, she would be able to play out enough rope for him to hang himself.

"I'd appreciate it if you'd come up to my apartment," Alana said. "I've...I'm sorry, Bill. What you said about forgiveness—I realize that you are right. I've been wrong. If I want to be forgiven myself, then I have to be willing to forgive others. I want to. I really do," she said.

Alana had intended to mouth the disarming words simply to get Bill off her back, but as she said them, a torrent of hurt and pain from the past came flooding back. Although she didn't want to take Bill into her confidence, the words started flowing.

"I hurt so bad when you walked out on me, Bill, and at times I hurt almost as bad now that you've walked back into my life. A part of me wants to forgive you, but another part of me wants to hate you forever!"

She regarded him with eyes brimming with tears.

"I love it, Pet," he said, laughing softly. "You're getting honest. We were never honest with each other in the past."

"You sound like Carrie," Alana said, unable to allow herself to look at him.

Bill shrugged.

"Perhaps because Carrie and I have learned to trust God about everything." He touched Alana's cheek. "I hope someday to have your forgiveness given with a free and joyous heart—not just a sentiment offered because you feel it's socially appropriate or something that will help me feel better."

"At the moment, I don't think I can do it." Alana paused. "But if this means anything, part of me does want to someday be able to forgive you, Bill." *And forgive myself*, she added in her thoughts.

"Then that's a start," Bill said. "You're willing to be willing. And sometimes I think that's the first step to trusting Christ. Becoming willing to be willing when the time is right."

Alana made no reply, so Bill took her apartment key from her, unlocked the door, and closed it behind them.

"Well, I'm home safe and sound. You can go now."

Bill frowned. "First I'd like to check around if you don't mind."

"Something tells me you won't leave me alone until I agree. So go ahead," she gave a feeble gesture. "Look around to your heart's content."

"I'll only take a minute, and then you'll be rid of me."

"I'm going to check my answering machine for messages," Alana said.

"I can see myself out," Bill agreed.

"Thank you for the ride," Alana said formally, aware of how suddenly old barriers had sprung between them just when they had started to be honest with each other.

The light indicator on the machine blinked several times. There were several hang-up calls, but that wasn't unusual. Many of Alana's friends simply didn't like to speak to a machine and would hang up and try later. The final call was a crank call. Alana hurriedly turned down the volume, hoping that Bill hadn't heard, but when she heard a floorboard creak, she realized that he had.

"What's going on, Lannie?"

She decided not to try to brazen it out with a carefree bluff. Even so, she took a long time to choose her words.

"I don't know. I've been trying to figure it out, but I'm so confused. So frightened."

Bill was across the room in a pace. His arm went around her shoulder.

"Are you frightened to the point where you're ready to get honest and tell me all that's been going on in your life?"

Alana thought it over. She knew that there were risks in keeping silent and risks in deciding to trust Bill. She had read quite a lot of Scripture lately and listened to Carrie at length on different occasions. It seemed that Bill Sterling no longer made up the rules as he went along. Instead he was patterning his life after a set of ethical principles ordained by God.

"It might be a long story," Alana said. "I'm at the point where I need to talk to someone. You're here. You're handy. I guess that makes you it. So if you've got the time,

I do, too."

"Lord willing, I'll have the rest of my life to listen to you," Bill murmured under his breath so low that Alana did not hear. A moment later, he drew her slowly, gently, toward him, intent on kissing away her fears.

She weakened, wanting to be in his arms, but at that instant the telephone shrilled. She caught herself and quickly edged away from Bill to answer the phone.

He drew her close again, gently capturing her in his loving arms.

"Let the machine get it," he whispered, his strong grip encircling her wrist.

Alana tugged away, but he restrained her, so she cocked her head to hear the message that would come after the electronic beep.

"Fool!" a harsh, grating voice rasped. "Bill Sterling is not your friend, you little idiot. He's a master of disguise. Beware lest the enemy invade you unawares."

Alana froze.

"Oh no—another one!" Alana cried, anguished.

"Another? How many of these have you had?" Bill asked.

"Four today."

"And you couldn't—wouldn't—talk about this before? Why?"

"Because I wasn't sure whom I should tell."

"You can do better than that, Pet. You could've talked to me. To Carrie. To Mark. And certainly to the police."

"I did talk to the police. Weeks ago. It did no good."

Without needing explanations, Bill slammed his fist onto the desk beside the telephone.

"Confounded red tape!" he snapped.

"Bill, don't get so upset. I'm sure it's really nothing. I'll be okay. The person will tire of me."

Bill shook his head. "This isn't a random call, Alana. It appears that not only do you have an enemy, but I do, as well."

"But who?" Alana inquired.

"That remains for us to figure out," Bill said in a grim tone. "With the police—or without them." He drew out his pocket recorder and produced his note pad and pen. He gave Alana a curt nod, all business, all professionalism.

"All right, ma'am," he drawled softly. "Tell me what's been going on. Start at the beginning. And don't leave out any detail—no matter how small or inconsequential it may seem."

As if she had no will of her own, Alana began talking, stating facts, dates, times, and strategic information as accurately as she could recall it.

But as she did, she wondered once again if Bill was her enemy or her protector. The more she thought it over, the more confused she became. Was it possible that he was trying to accomplish with fear what he'd been unable to manage on his own? Instead of loving her back to him, was Bill Sterling intent on scaring her into his arms?

seventeen

Alana spoke on until her voice grew tired, and still Bill barraged her with questions that proved that as a private investigator he would be among the best. He left no stone unturned in his search for information, and it was clear that he explored random possibilities to isolate who should be included in the rogues' gallery of suspects—and what might be their motives.

In spite of this, Alana didn't let herself forget that Bill was an excellent actor. If he intended to disarm her, he would play the part of the get-tough investigator to the hilt, leaving no angle unpursued.

"Our best piece of evidence is the surveillance car. Hopefully, I'll be able to reach my contact this afternoon. Once we get an ID on the auto's owner, this case could become a piece of cake."

Alana wondered if the car would be back in a rental agency's parking lot come evening, and if then, Bill would feel he could safely continue to watch her.

"What happens when we know?" Alana asked, playing along with what she realized might be his game.

Bill shrugged. "I go have a little talk with the person who's been sitting in the car staking you out."

"And then?"

"Either I'll know we're barking up the wrong tree, or I'll

know we have the right suspect and issue a few make-my-day ultimatums. If that fails, we'll involve the various law agencies. If we can link up the evidence of the crank calls, dead flowers, and other forms of behavior that constitute harassment charges, we'll have something to go with."

"I want you to catch the person," Alana said, "but a part of me fears it, too."

"Don't be frightened, Alana, but be sensible. I don't want you staying here alone. I want you to pack an overnight bag, and I'm going to see if you can stay with Carrie or with Mark and his parents." His attitude was dead serious.

"Bill, aren't you overreacting?" Alana admonished, giving him a chance to come clean and admit that perhaps in reality the situation wasn't as bad as he was making it out to be.

He gave her a tired smile and smoothed her blond hair away from her troubled eyes. "Hey, Pet, which one of us does this for a living?"

"Okay," Alana agreed. "But can you give me a while?"

"Only a little while."

"But I have so many things to do."

"Sweetheart, so do I."

"Could you maybe run a few of your errands and then come back for me? That'd give me a chance to do the things I have to, and give you the time you need to put things in motion."

Bill thought it over.

"Okay. I guess so. Lock the door after me, and don't open up for anyone else. Oh!" He dug into his pocket and extracted a pretty bracelet. "I want you to wear this. Don't take it off."

She looked at it. It looked like a bracelet of exquisite design and craftsmanship, nothing more.

"Don't take it off, huh?" she inquired lightly.

"Right."

She was about to chide him by calling him James Bond or asking, How gullible do you think I am? But she decided that such responses would reveal her distrust. She managed to keep a straight face as Bill fit the bracelet onto her left wrist.

"Now don't take it off," he admonished.

"Righto," she agreed, but a moment later Alana gave a wry laugh. "You've watched too many PI shows on television, Bill."

Bill gave her a mystified grin.

"And you, my dear, may not have watched enough of them. Now do as you're told. Remember: I love you, Alana. Lord willing, I will not allow harm to befall you."

"Run and do your errands," Alana replied.

"Be ready when I get back. I'll call Mark or Carrie from the car phone."

No sooner was Bill out the door and en route to the elevator than Alana secured all the locks on her apartment door. She flew about her tasks. She laid out clothes for the next day; gathered her toiletries, cosmetics, blow-dryer, curling iron, and nightwear; and hastily packed everything into a suitcase.

Her family Bible was on the night table beside the bed, and on impulse she placed it with her belongings, giving added heft to the small overnight case.

As she worked, Alana reviewed the afternoon's conversation and became more convinced than ever that Bill's performance was just that: an act. She considered leaving on her own, checking into a hotel, and not being there when Bill returned. He was following a set pattern: first he talked of her fright, and then he assured her of his love. Alana was becoming increasingly certain that her suspicions were correct and that Bill was attempting to scare her into his arms.

She was rushing around the apartment, making sure everything was turned off when the telephone rang. As unnerved as she was, she almost answered, but as she reached for the phone, she remembered to let the machine screen for her. It would probably be wiser to let her caller think she wasn't home.

Alana stood beside the answering machine, heart thudding, and waited what seemed like an eternity for the machine to beep and the caller to speak. She prayed fervently that the caller would be Bill, Carrie, or some friend from the community theater.

"I know you're there, little fool! Soon, I will be, too, for I'll be arriving to get you. I've waited for you to come to me, but time has run out. Prepare yourself for my coming."

Frantically Alana disengaged the answering machine

and dialed Bill's number. She knew that she'd been wrong—all wrong—and that Bill was as innocent and as trustworthy as he had acted. It had been her own attitudes and animosities that had prevented her from meeting truth with truth. He had spoken honestly, but she had viewed everything through the screen of distrust.

Alana prayed that she would reach Bill, but he did not answer either at his apartment or office. She didn't know the number on his car phone, so she left a message on his answering machine at home, uncertain that it would make any sense to him.

In desperation she hit the auto-dial button for Carrie. Carrie's machine came on. Alana almost cried in frustration and fear, but she left a message in case Carrie was at home and screening her calls.

Then she remembered that Carrie would likely be with Mark and his parents. She fumbled, angry over her impatience, as she tried to find the telephone number for Mark's parents in the directory.

The phone rang and rang before Mark's mother answered. In a hysterical voice Alana asked for Mark or Carrie. It seemed to take forever for someone to pick up the receiver.

Alana heard the whining of the elevator down the hall as it rose from the lobby. Her heartbeat increased to a jackhammer cadence. Somehow, she knew, she just knew that it was her tormenter, coming for her.

"At least there are the locks between us," she whispered. "Oh, Lord. Protect me now," she whispered. "My life is in

Your hands."

"Mark Landry, here." He answered the telephone as if he expected to find a client on the line.

Alana's voice was strident with terror.

"Mark, it's me, Alana! Bill just left. But I'm being harassed, getting crank calls. There've been unpleasant happenings in my life. Bill plans to take me to a safe place. I—we—thought I'd be safe. But...but the man called back, and he's on his way to get me—"

"Calm down, dear," Mark said. "I'll call 9-1-1. You're going to be okay. You have a good security system. Don't unlock for anyone!"

"I won't!" she vowed, even as she heard what sounded like keys being tested in the locks. "Wait—Mark, he's trying keys in my locks!"

"Easy, Lannie. Chances of someone having the right combination for all of your locks are almost nil. Do you have a chain lock on your door?"

"Oh, no! I forgot to hook that!" Alana cried.

She dropped the receiver, ran to the door, and at that instant the series of locks lined up, the handle rotated, and the door swung open. Alana felt dizzy. The room spun, and she fell backward. Just before she hit the floor, someone caught her. Alana looked up into a sinister face made even more terrifying because it was covered with a woman's black nylon stocking. It was almost impossible to make out the man's features.

"No! Please!" Alana cried as her attacker wrestled with her.

He clamped a foul-smelling cloth across her face. Even as she struggled, she felt her mind being pulled down, down, down into a dark abyss. The attacker lifted her limp body up and ran with her down the hall and into the waiting elevator.

Alana tried to cry for help, but all that she could muster was a faint croak. The day had been glaringly gray, but with a muffled thump everything grew black. Alana pitched about. Groggily she realized that she was inside a trunk, going who knew where, with a madman whose identity Bill desperately needed to discover. She groped frantically around in the dark, trying to free the trunk lid. After several failed attempts, she fell back, exhausted.

As the miles rushed past, Alana started thinking. She remembered the pastor's sermon that morning. Her thoughts flew back to the Sunday school class when they had talked about the Lord's protection. She dwelled on things others had said as they talked about purpose in life. So many things—so many comforting ideas came to her mind. Gradually she began to lose her fear of the unknown and began to understand one thing: God knew, loved, and cared about her.

The Lord knew that she had been abducted, but He would not abandon her. He would use Bill and other people to come to her rescue. And if they were too late, God would bring good out of the tragedy.

Years ago, He had wept with a little girl whose parents had died. Although she had felt deserted, God had been with her every step of the way. He had brought her loving family and friends and many opportunities to return to Him. Tears of healing trickled down Alana's cheeks.

"You are the Redeemer," she whispered in prayer. "Thank You for Your love and care. I'll trust You with whatever happens."

With that thought in her mind, lulled by the rhythm of the road, Alana drifted off to sleep, knowing that soon she would need to be awake, refreshed, and strong.

eighteen

Alana did not sleep for long. When she woke, she was unsure of what direction the car was traveling in until her ears began to pop. It was likely that her kidnapper had gone through South County and into the Little Ozark area of southeastern Missouri, not far from the bluffs overlooking the Mississippi River.

The area had some caves, both explored and uncharted, that were reminiscent of the upriver area near Hannibal, made famous by Mark Twain's stories about Tom Sawyer and Huck Finn.

On and on the car traveled. After a while, Alana's ears began to feel more comfortable, and she knew that they had passed through the Little Ozark area. She was starting to feel nauseated by the fuel fumes. Diesel smoke almost gagged her when they were on the freeway. The pitching of the car as the driver zoomed in and out of traffic pushed her to the edge in her constant battle against being violently ill in the close, dark confines of the musty trunk.

She didn't know how she could endure another mile of riding, but somehow she did, and she prayed that God would deliver her from the torment. Just when she was wondering if she would ride on in a trunk for ever, the car slowed and swerved. Then Alana felt the climb as the large automobile nosed upward. Pebbles peppered the underside of the car, creating a deafening roar.

As soon as the car hit level ground, it rolled to a smooth stop, and the engine turned off. In the sudden quiet, Alana could hear the birds in nearby trees chatter in alarm over the intrusion of their domain.

The car door opened. Steps crunched on the gravel. A key clicked as it was inserted in the trunk lock. The mechanism turned. A crack of daylight appeared before the lid was thrown open. Late afternoon sunlight blinded Alana.

She'd expected to confront sinister features. Instead she saw Gordon Walters.

"Gordon?" Alana spluttered. "How? What?"

Gordon gave a sinister grin.

"It was a piece of cake, you trusting little fool. The night of Mother's dinner party, I met you and parked your car while the butler ushered you into the house with the other guests. You entrusted your key ring to me. With special wax, I made imprints of all of your keys and had a locksmith create duplicates. You couldn't keep yourself inviolate from me. I had access to you any time I wanted."

Stricken, Alana realized how she had mistrusted Bill Sterling, who had tried to show her by word, act, and deed that he was a changed man, while she had not bothered to be cautious with Gordy, a man about whom she knew so little.

"Welcome to Briarwood Estates, my love," Gordy said, as if he had borne her to a palace in a sumptuous conveyance. He bowed low.

Alana thought of grabbing for the tire iron that had
gouged her during the ride, hitting him over the head with
it, and knocking him unconscious long enough to tie him
up and drive for help. Just then Gordy opened his eyes and
stretched out a courtly hand to help her out of the trunk.
The moment—and her opportunity—were lost.

"Whose place is this?" Alana asked, stumbling as she
tried to become accustomed to standing.

"Ours. Mother's and mine. When she dies, it will be all
mine." Gordy recounted how the antebellum mansion had
been built when slaves worked the fields and had been in
the Walters family since before the Civil War.

Alana hoped that if she could get him talking about the
architecture, he would become more docile. Perhaps she
could handle him as deftly as she usually did at community
theater gatherings.

"And this is where my ancestors confined their recalci-
trant slaves," Gordy said, showing her a dungeon-like
room that had hooks and chains secured into the stone and
mortar walls. "Here's where they awaited the arrival of
slave traders to take them to auction for resale. Bad slaves
stayed here, and there was no escape."

"How awful," Alana said, shuddering.

Gordy looked around.

"Not really awful at all. I think it could be fixed up quite
comfortably." He looked at her with eyes that were too
bright. "'Peter, Peter, pumpkin eater, had a wife and
couldn't keep her.' I couldn't keep you, either. Peter kept

his wife in a pumpkin. Guess where I'm going to keep you, my darling girl? You'll never go to Bill Sterling again. Nor will he come to you."

"Oh yes he will!" Alana angrily cried. "He's checking on you right now. He'll arrive to rescue me—and he'll have police, federal marshals, whatever it takes."

In response, Gordon chuckled.

"Laugh," Alana invited. "But you're destined to fail, Gordon. Bill always does what he says he will. He's promised to protect me. He won't let me down. And even if he were to be stymied in his efforts, I'm under the protection of my Lord and Savior, Jesus Christ. You can't lift so much as a finger to harm me, Gordon, unless the Lord allows it. And if the Lord allows it, I willingly follow in service to Him. I belong to Him."

"No!" Gordy cried in protest, his voice hoarse. "You belong to me. I've loved you. I've adored you. I won't share you with another. If I can't have you—no one will."

"I belong to the Lord, Gordy. And I love Bill Sterling. I always liked you only as my friend, and now you're betraying my trust. But it's not too late. Please don't do this to yourself or to me. God doesn't want you to do things that separate you from Him."

Suddenly, Alana knew what Bill had tried to tell her. Renewed through the Lord, given life in Him, he was changed and reborn a different man. One who felt, thought, and reacted in new and better ways.

From a strictly human viewpoint, she had plenty of reason to hate, fear, and scorn Gordy. But now that she was committed to obeying and trusting the Lord, He gave her the strength to feel compassion for Gordy. While she abhorred what Gordy was doing to her, she cared for his soul. Just as Bill had said he'd pray for the people who caused misfortune to people like Missy, so did Alana want Gordon to be willing to accept forgiveness and love from God.

"I won't share you. I don't care what Mother says about sharing!" Gordon blurted out, sounding like a petulant little boy who resented the rules of social conduct. "I shan't share you with anyone. And that's that!"

With a rough gesture, Gordon shoved Alana into the cubical and slammed the door shut, slipping the lock home with a clang of finality that seemed to echo through the ages.

Alana considered the stories that had been discussed in church and Sunday school about prisoners. Often, the Lord had provided miraculous escapes for them, including the stone rolling away from the tomb on Easter Sunday as Christ triumphed over the bonds of death.

The winter sun was setting, and Alana could see the shadows lengthen. She thought that she heard the car drive away, but she couldn't be sure. Nighttime came. It grew colder. She shivered helplessly and was reduced to calling out Gordon's name, pleading with him to come to her. Only eerie silence answered her.

Alana cried out until she was hoarse and her loudest sound became a faint croak. Finally she lay down and wept. Helplessness surged through her, but at the moment of greatest despair, the strength of the Lord flowed into her, seeming to warm her body as well as her spirit.

"Thy will be done," she whispered as she drifted off to sleep. She stayed huddled in a ball to conserve her heat, and her left hand rested in a relaxed caress on the gold bracelet that Bill had given her.

Alana had studied that bracelet while there was still light. It had seemed too tiny to be any kind of transmitter, but with modern technology, almost anything was possible. Perhaps it wasn't a homing device with which they could locate her, but it gave her some reason to remain optimistic.

Periodically Alana woke during the night. She saw proof of the Lord's protection when a strong wind rushed up from the south, bringing with it a tide of unseasonably warm air from the Gulf and making the room more tolerable.

As the sun rose, Alana became aware of how hungry and thirsty she was. Stuffing her hand into her jacket pocket to get warm, she found the little tract that she'd slipped into her pocket at church the day before. She didn't have food for her body, but the Lord was feeding her spirit.

Alana kept glancing at her watch, but that only made time stand still. To get her mind off the cold and the waiting, she started praying.

She was so focused on her prayers that at first she didn't notice sounds coming from the knoll where the old mansion was located. When she did, she wasn't sure whether to feel fear or relief. Was Gordy returning, or was someone trying to rescue her?

Alana's heart surged with hope as she determined that there was too much noise being created for it to be from only one person. Then she heard different voices calling her name. She sensed that the group was moving quickly but with thorough deliberation.

"Bill! Bill—I'm here! Oh, darling, please hurry—hurry!" she cried. She wanted to sob when she realized that the wind carried her voice away from the group.

Looking through a crack in the door, Alana could detect movement halfway up the hill. When the rescue team veered away, Alana moaned in anguish, but suddenly the group turned back. She saw team members consult some type of device with antennas, looked at the bracelet Bill had given her, and became convinced it was sending out a signal for them. Bill was coming for her!

Even though the wind was against her, Alana started yelling again, continuing on long after she grew hoarse. Bill heard her and motioned to the others. They swarmed toward Alana like a hive of bees in their eagerness to help.

The door to the dungeon was locked securely. Bill told Alana to stand in the near corner, facing the wall. He took a pistol from his shoulder holster and with two quick shots demolished the padlock. The chain clanked free.

Almost before it seemed possible, the door swung open, and as Alana stumbled from the slave dungeon into the morning light, Bill rushed forward and crushed her in his arms.

"How did you find me?" she asked. "I guessed this

bracelet had to contain a homing device, but I'm sure it doesn't have a large range. You had to have been within a certain radius to pick up the signal."

Bill nodded.

"I traced the license plate before I found out from Mark that you had disappeared. We contacted the authorities immediately and gave them the information we had. The car is owned by Mrs. Sheffield-Walters. Gordy had his own car that he drove to play practice, but he had free usage of his mother's car when she wasn't in need of transportation. That's why you never knew that he had access to a car that was a duplicate for mine, and that it was he—not me—who was stalking you.

"The police tried reaching Mrs. Sheffield-Waters at her home, but she was away for the weekend, and Gordy was nowhere to be found. By the time they managed to track down Mrs. Sheffield-Waters, it was close to midnight.

"She likes you very much, Alana. She believed you'd be a wonderful influence on Gordon. She hoped for the best—that you'd get him settled down. Under question-ing, she finally admitted she's had problems with Gordon. When Gordon got into trouble as a teenager, his late father applied money to the right places, and the boy was forgiven his pranks. As an adult it has become more serious. Even sinister.

"We asked Mrs. Sheffield-Waters where she thought Gordon might be. She suggested this place as well as another area closer to home. We checked that location first and found Gordon. He surrendered peacefully."

"What are they going to do to him?" Alana inquired.

"He's in the care of his family physician and his psychiatrist. He was rehospitalized early this morning. He will be kept under supervision even after his hospitalization ends. He'll get the help he needs. His mother, and the authorities, will see to it."

"Oh, Bill. How awful!"

"Don't feel bad about it, Alana. It's for the best. Gordon's getting the help he needs, and that should prevent future tragedy. He confessed to cutting the brake line on Missy's car. He had such a warped view of his relationship with you that he felt her supposed triumph over you was actually a victory over himself. He sought his sick revenge, but she's going to be well.

"Now you're safe, and he's going to be healed. Don't be upset, Pet. It could've been so much worse. He could've held you hostage. He could've been faced with federal marshals or a fatal shoot-out."

Alana shuddered. "You're right. But you know, Bill, I never did feel that I was in mortal danger."

"Of course not. You were in the Lord's protection."

"Yes, and yours, my love. My trustworthy beloved."

"Do you mean that?"

"More than you'll ever know."

"Then I think we should make it official, Pet. I'd like to place you under my protection permanently. How about it?"

"I'd like that."

"Then will you become my wife?"

"I can't wait to say, 'I do.' "

Bill gave her a slow and thorough kiss.

"Still sure you want to become Mrs. Bill Sterling?"

"Even more certain than I was a moment before. I know that from the very first moments of creation, ours was a love meant to be. And Bill Sterling, that assurance from the Lord is good enough for me!"

A Letter To Our Readers

Dear Reader:

In order that we might better contribute to your reading enjoyment, we would appreciate your taking a few minutes to respond to the following questions. When completed, please return to the following:

Karen Carroll, Editor
Heartsong Presents
P.O. Box 719
Uhrichsville, Ohio 44683

1. Did you enjoy reading *A Love Meant to Be*?
   ☐ Very much. I would like to see more books
      by this author!
   ☐ Moderately
      I would have enjoyed it more if _____

   _____

2. Are you a member of *Heartsong Presents*? Yes   No
   If no, where did you purchase this book? _____

   _____

3. What influenced your decision to purchase
   this book? (Circle those that apply.)

Cover	Back cover copy
Title	Friends
Publicity	Other _____

4. On a scale from 1 (poor) to 10 (superior), please rate the following elements.

___Heroine   ___Plot

___Hero   ___Inspirational theme

___Setting   ___Secondary characters

5. What settings would you like to see covered in *Heartsong Presents* books?

_____

_____

6. What are some inspirational themes you would like to see treated in future books?_____

_____

_____

7. Would you be interested in reading other *Heartsong Presents* titles?   Yes   No

8. Please circle your age range:
   Under 18   18-24   25-34
   35-45   46-55   Over 55

9. How many hours per week do you read? _____

Name _____

Occupation _____

Address _____

City _____ State _____ Zip _____

The "Miranda Trilogy"
by Grace Livingston Hill

Great New Inspirational Fiction

from HEART♥NG PRESENTS

Biblical Novel Collection #1

by Lee Webber

<u>Two complete inspirational novels in one volume.</u>

_____ **BNC1 CALL ME SARAH**—Can Sarah, like Queen Esther be used by God . . . even as a slave in Herod's place?
CAPERNAUM CENTURION—One Centurion's life is irrevocably changed by his encounter with a certain Nazarene.

Citrus County Mystery Collection #1

by Mary Carpenter Reid

<u>Two complete inspirational mystery and romance novels in one volume.</u>

_____ **CCM1 TOPATOPA**—Can Alyson Kendricks make an historic village come alive . . . without becoming history herself?
DRESSED FOR DANGER—Roxanne Shelton's fashion designs were the key to her success . . . but did they unlock a closet of secrets?

BOTH COLLECTIONS ARE AVAILABLE FOR $3.97 EACH THROUGH HEARTSONG PRESENTS. ORIGINALLY PUBLISHED AT $7.95 EACH.

Send to: Heartsong Presents Reader's Service
P.O. Box 719
Uhrichsville, Ohio 44683

Please send me the items checked above. I am enclosing
$_____ (please add $1.00 to cover postage and handling).
Send check or money order, no cash or C.O.D.s, please.
To place a credit card order, call 1-800-847-8270.

NAME _____

ADDRESS _____

CITY / STATE _____ ZIP _____
BNC1/CCMC1

LOVE A GREAT LOVE STORY?

Introducing Heartsong Presents —
Your Inspirational Book Club

Heartsong Presents Christian romance reader's service will provide you with four never before published romance titles every month! In fact, your books will be mailed to you at the same time advance copies are sent to book reviewers. You'll preview each of these new and unabridged books before they are released to the general public.

These books are filled with the kind of stories you have been longing for—stories of courtship, chivalry, honor, and virtue. Strong characters and riveting plot lines will make you want to read on and on. Romance is not dead, and each of these romantic tales will remind you that Christian faith is still the vital ingredient in an intimate relationship filled with true love and honest devotion.

Sign up today to receive your first set. Send no money now. We'll bill you only $9.97 post-paid with your shipment. Then every month you'll automatically receive the latest four "hot off the press" titles for the same low post-paid price of $9.97. That's a savings of 50% off the $4.95 cover price. When you consider the exaggerated shipping charges of other book clubs, your savings are even greater!

THERE IS NO RISK—you may cancel at any time without obligation. And if you aren't completely satisfied with any selection, return it for an immediate refund.

TO JOIN, just complete the coupon below, mail it today, and get ready for hours of wholesome entertainment.

Now you can curl up, relax, and enjoy some great reading full of the warmhearted spirit of romance.